GREAT WHITE HOUSE

Christoph Paul
&
Arthur Graham
&
Brody Thomas

The book is dedicated to all of the hard workers at the NSA.
Please do not arrest us.

PART 1

Chapter 1

Washington, D.C. The White House

Most stories should not begin with "It was a dark and stormy night," but this particular evening could not be described in any other way. A great storm was raging outside the White House, as were the key political figures sheltered within. The nation's top leaders had gathered in the East Room, and were bickering amongst themselves while they waited for the Chinese President's call.

The matter under discussion tonight? The massive debt owed to his country.

Present at the table were those elite few with direct access to the recently re-elected President Obama and Vice President Biden. It would have been any news reporter's dream to sit alongside these political heavyweights, but the China Task Force (CTF for short) had made this a closed conference, top-secret event. So secret, in fact, that not even Edward Snowden could've possibly known about it.

Even if the White House had allowed the press to attend, it was doubtful that the reporters could have made it through the torrential downpour hammering on Washington that night. Hurricane-force winds battered the entire city, and visibility on the flooded streets had dropped close to zero. All traffic had ceased hours earlier as government employees hunkered down in their favorite bars and strip clubs to weather out the storm.

The mood in the room grew ever more tense while they waited for President Jinping to appear onscreen.

"I just don't trust these dang Chinese," Minnesota Representative Michele Bachmann said. "Even with their food. My husband ends up having rectal problems every time he eats it while I'm away. You should see the fees I pay his proctologist.... Thank the good Lord we don't have ObamaCare, or he'd probably never crap right again!"

The other members of the CTF remained quiet, as most believed Mr. Bachmann to be a closeted homosexual. Ever the peacemaker, President Obama sought to avoid any divisive issues being brought to the table. "Yes, Congresswoman Bachmann," he said. "I understand. Chinese food, though delicious, often bothers my stomach and my wife's stomach as well."

It was then that Vice President Biden rose from his seat, heading for the decanter on a nearby sideboard. "Hey Barry," he said to Obama, checking his watch. "I thought it was you black guys who were supposed to be late all the time, not the Chinese. Ha!"

The oft-amused Biden chuckled to himself as he poured another drink. President Obama could only shake his head in response, grateful that the press hadn't been there to catch this latest 'JoeGaffe'. Returning to the table with the decanter in hand, Biden sipped his scotch and Obama popped another piece of Nicorette into his mouth.

"Since this meeting is 'not official'," the Vice President continued, "I suppose it's all right for us to have a few drinks." He poured another glass for Wisconsin Representative Paul Ryan, seated there beside him. The two of them had become close since their recent Vice Presidential debate, and would often drink together while discussing the 'malarkey' of the day.

Meanwhile, House Majority Leader Eric Cantor was fed up with their joking and shenanigans. "In all seriousness," he began, seated beside Speaker of the House John Boehner, "what the Chinese President is doing here is a power play. It's a psychological display of dominance. You just can't trust a Communist to play things straight with you."

Texas Senator Ted Cruz abruptly slammed his fist onto the table. "Those commies will play mind games!" he said. "I totally agree...."

House Minority Leader Nancy Pelosi politely raised her hand. "Excuse me, gentlemen," she said, "but I for one am much more worried about this storm going on. We might be stuck here all night!" She gestured to the window. "It's gotten dangerous out there, I'm telling you. Only global warming could cause a downpour of this magnitude; my constituents are very worried about this issue and so am I."

Democratic LDS Senator Harry Reid and Socialist Bernie Sanders expressed their agreement, while Congresswoman Bachmann and Congressman Tim Scott both mouthed silent prayers for the misguided heathens in the room. The other Republicans simply rolled their eyes at Pelosi's pandering statement.

Libertarian-leaning Senator Rand Paul wasn't so inclined to let it go, however. "If global warming even exists," he responded, "the market will fix it."

Federal Reserve Chairman Ben Bernanke and former Secretary of the Treasury Timothy Geithner (called out of retirement to help the CTF) nodded in approval of his sensible market solution.

President Obama took a deep breath and offered a fake but sincere-appearing smile to acknowledge Paul's statement. The assembled policy makers continued their squabbling amongst themselves until he finally raised a hand to quiet the room.

"Now, now," he began, "let's not have the global warming debate again, folks. Not tonight. In times like this, it's important that we stay focused on the issue at hand."

"But what exactly is the issue at hand?" asked House Speaker Boehner. "Why do we all have to be here so late, just because President Jinping says so?"

President Obama cleared his throat. "The Chinese government may be concerned about our mounting debt," he replied, "but that is not the only reason for our emergency meeting here tonight. I regret to inform you that the NSA has picked up some terrorist chatter about a potential attack on our nation's naval bases, one that could easily cripple an entire fleet. According to our best available intel, the Chinese may have something to do with it."

For once, he had their full attention.

"We might be in for a long night," he continued. "Look, if this storm gets any worse, you all can just crash here; it's a big house, after all. We can sell to it to the press as a bipartisan pajama party. You know they'll have themselves a field day with that one."

New York Senator Charles Schumer winced as he rubbed his weary temples. "Oi vey," he groaned, "I don't have my Ambien with me...."

Senator Claire McCaskill gave him a nice Missouri smile. "It's okay, Chuck," she said, "You can have some of mine. Marco, I have some bottled water too, if you need it."

The group shared a laugh at Florida Senator Rubio's expense as he bristled at the overused joke, but somehow he managed an affable grin that only a man running for President in 2016 was capable of pulling off.

It was then that Arizona Senator John McCain quit the poker game he'd been playing with one of the Secret Service agents. "You pansies and your goddamn sleeping pills," he said. "When I was in Vietnam, I slept on pure steel and spider shit. President Obama, sir, I'm sick of waiting for these Communists to call. Either you ring them up or I will."

President Obama glanced around the room, gauging the rising levels of annoyance and frustration. At times like this he was positively fed up with being President, but he knew better than to indulge in that kind of self-pity. He just looked out the window at the worsening storm, thinking of his Kenyan father, imagining him herding goats in this weather. His father was a strong man, and would not have been deterred by hardships like this.

By and by, the President sighed with grim resignation. "All right, John," he said. "Enough is enough. Let's get President Jinping onscreen. Might as well get this over with."

President Obama politely shushed the gathered members of the CTF, reaching for the communications console before him. With his finger poised above the call button, a tremendous lightning bolt erupted from the sky, illuminating the terrified faces of all in attendance.

The President gave one last look around the table, gulped and pressed the little green button.

Click.

The mood in the room grew tense when President Jinping appeared onscreen.

Sporting a black, gaudily embroidered changshan, he was seated upon an ornate golden throne, languidly stroking the pretty white cat in his lap as he grinned from ear to ear. He reminded several of the Senators present of Leslie Chow, the Chinese caricature from The Hangover.

Congresswoman Bachmann (unfamiliar with that particular

film herself) gasped as she grabbed the arm of Senator Ted Cruz, seated to her left. "I heard they eat them!" she whispered loudly in his ear. "That's probably his breakfast..."

Unperturbed, President Jinping continued petting his cat. "Not true, Mrs. Bachmann," he said. "I afraid you have us confused with the Koreans."

"No, I heard it my prayer group," she said, "I'm not going to fall for your Communist lies! Oh dear, that poor cat...."

President Obama raised his hand. "Please, Congresswoman Bachmann, let us show some respect to President Jinping."

"It okay, President Obama. She not know no better," the Chinese leader replied. "Her YouTube videos very popular in China.... As you know, we block most Internet, but still let hers in for entertainment purpose." Jinping continued running his fingers through the cat's fluffy fur. "If you really must know, Congresswoman Bachmann, China actually has plans to adopt nationwide, mandatory vegan diet."

Bachmann just shook her head with added disgust. "That sounds about right, you bunch of wall-building pansies," she said. "And would you please stop putting so much MSG in your General Tso's chicken while you're at it? It causes great problems for my husband's rectal health. Maybe you should be paying me, huh?"

Taking the higher road, the Chinese President tactfully declined mentioning Mr. Bachmann's rumored homosexuality.

"We are not, as you say, pansies," he began. "We are very disciplined people and lovers of all animals. For example, I love this cat. Perhaps you would you like to know her name?"

"Sure," Eric Cantor indulged the Chinese president.

President Jinping's face turned bright red as he tried to suppress a laugh. "Trillion Dollar Debt!" he finally guffawed, slapping his knee as the storm over D.C. grew stronger.

The thunder was so loud now on the American side of the teleconference, it spooked the cat on the Chinese side, prompting it to jump off the President's lap. Jinping nonchalantly brushed its fur from his changshan. "I hear the weather is quite deadly in Washington tonight," he said, "almost... unnatural, wouldn't you say? Perhaps it like your capitalist economy—not functioning properly?"

"The weather is acting rather strange tonight," Obama replied, trying to take control of the conversation, "but it doesn't help that your carbon emissions have surpassed our own lately."

"Do not change subject, President Obama. We want to be clean; we have great plans for China, but my economic czars tell me we need funding for these great plans, and we cannot fund them until your debt is paid. In full."

"President Jinping...."

"Need back now!" The Chinese President exploded, gesticulating wildly at the camera. "You pay now! You pay now, Obama! Your democracy move too slow. Always spending money on wars, and no even win! We want pay now!"

"Now, now," Obama replied to his tirade. "There's no need to raise your voice. Our nation is hurting economically at this time, you understand. We just had a recession. We're still trying to recover from it, and now you're acting like sharks with blood in the water all of a sudden."

"Good choice of words, President Obama," the Chinese President replied, calming down as a mischievous smile crept across his lips. "I believe your English term is... foreshadowing?"

"Look, let's be civil here," President Obama continued, ignoring his vague threat. "There's absolutely no need for that kind of talk. We both have nukes. We can't have any talk of war—not over debt, not in the twenty-first century. We are both strong, rational nations."

"We no want war, Mr. President," Jinping said soothingly. "Nor do we wish harm to global community. Nuclear war would spell our mutual destruction, as you know. But unless you pay money owed, China must punish you; it is Chinese lesson that thieves must pay when they steal—they must pay back debt or meet white demon. It is in the Tao... I think. Probably. Either way, today is day you learn this lesson, or you too shall perish!"

Obama's brows knit themselves into a deep furrow as a single drop of sweat ran slowly down his cheek. "Let me be clear, President Jinping," he began, "I don't like where this conversation is going. Not one bit. Congress and I are doing the best we can to figure out this debt situation, and your extortionist tactics here tonight are not helping matters."

"Your best not good enough!" the Chinese President laughed. "We are beating your country in science and math; we soon be new super power. We have great power. Only conspiracy men on radio and Internet know truth. We can do things no one would believe!"

Jinping paused, raising an eyebrow for dramatic effect as another boom of thunder shook the White House.

"What the hell is this guy even talking about?" interjected Vice President Biden.

"I tell you what I talking about!" President Jinping continued. "Control... of weather. Yes, it is true—China has discovered glorious secret to weather control! While your nation watch football and sex tapes, we study! While you eat hamburger, we eat fish, which very good for brain."

Grinning like a madman, the Chinese President then held up what looked a giant remote control. "You will like this!" he squealed, cackling as he pressed a button.

Chapter 2

The screen then switched to show various parts of the city, many of them already under several feet of water. As the storm over Washington grew even stronger still, an image of the White House came onscreen, just barely visible through impenetrable sheets of rain.

When the Chinese President next appeared on camera, he wore a triumphant smirk upon his close-up face.

"We must give you some credit," he spoke over the roaring thunder, his voice now choppy with interference. "We Chinese not 'creatives' like you, but love American cinema like X-Men 1 and 2. Our scientists were inspired by Halle Berry's African superpowers, learning to harness weather too through much great study."

"How is that even possible?!" cried President Obama, losing his cool under pressure.

"Soon," President Jinping continued, "your pathetic White House will be completely underwater! Ahahahhahaha...." The way he cackled with such confidence, many in the CTF were convinced he actually believed it.

"Why you goddamn commie bastards..." growled Senator McCain, shoving a defiant finger at the camera. "You won't get away with this!"

Joe Biden drank deeply from his glass of scotch. "John," he slurred, "when you're right, you're right." Then, turning to Obama, "I told you, Barry, we need to keep funding science, not your stupid fucking healthcare bill! How in the hell are we supposed to control the weather now?"

Senator McCain was not impressed with the Chinese leader's threats. "Do you have any idea how many naval bases there are around here?" he asked incredulously. "It floods, and we're on a ship or a chopper in half an hour tops!"

"It funny you should mention Navy, Senator McCain," Jinping said, clicking his remote once again. The screen then switched to show ships of every kind in various states of wreckage, seamen struggling to escape the mass of crucified cruisers and destroyed destroyers.

While the other members of the CTF gasped in shock, Biden just rolled his eyes and downed the rest of his scotch. "Looks fake to me. Like something out of a retarded-ass Michael Bay movie. Chinaman's tricks. I'm not falling for it!"

Meanwhile, President Obama wasn't feeling so sure. He didn't think it looked that fake at all.

"You... you bombed our ships..." he muttered, holding his head in his hands. "You must realize, sir, that this means war!"

Jinping solemnly placed a hand over his heart in response. "No bomb ships, I promise. Just bad weather. Big storm surge, you see? You no listen, do you, President Obama...."

"Let me be clear," Obama stammered, attempting to regain his composure. "You cannot control the weather. This is absolutely preposterous!"

The Chinese President remained calm. "Yes, most countries

will believe that, too. They will say it is global warming, hahaha.... Who would believe that we now control weather? But we do."

President Obama gradually pulled himself together. He had heard rumors of President Jinping being mentally unbalanced, much like another Communist leader, Kim Jong-un, but he had never expected anything like this. Clearly, they were dealing with a certified maniac.

"So, what's the plan then?" he scoffed at the Chinese leader. "You're going to try flooding us into paying our debt?"

Rand Paul pantomimed a jerk-off gesture at this, but it wasn't clear whether it was intended for Jinping or Obama.

Ignoring them both, Jinping placed the remote in his lap and reached over to the side, picking up a fine ceramic bowl. Casually taking a sip of what appeared to be shark fin soup, he then set the bowl back down on the table to his left.

The Chinese President daintily wiped his mouth with a pink, monogrammed napkin. "President Obama," he began at length, "your brain so limited for someone who study so much in school. Your community organizing did not lead you to think... what you Americans say... outside of box?"

"Now, now," Obama shot back, "let's not make things personal, Jinping. I understand that you are upset about the debt we owe, but we Americans are an honorable people, and we are committed to finding an equitable solution to this problem. I implore you to listen to reason here tonight."

"You are not honorable," Jinping replied coldly. "And you are very rude for not even asking how my meal tastes...."

Joe Biden nodded in agreement. "He's right. That does look pretty good, Jinping. I'm a pretty big fan of shark fin soup myself. I know a good spot in Delaware, but it's Mexican and—"

"Not now, Joe..." Obama sighed, raising a hand to quiet him.

"Thank you, Vice President Biden," Jinping replied. "What I am eating certainly does look like shark fin soup, a delicacy here in China, but I am afraid you are incorrect."

Biden wobbled slightly as he poured himself and Paul Ryan another scotch. "I'm telling ya, Barry, it's shark fin soup. Had it back in '09, when I visited them on that international relations tour you sent me on for some reason. I swear, that motherfucking shark fin soup tasted better than my second wife's—"

Obama cut him off. "Please, get to the point, President Jinping."

"It is true," the Chinese President continued, "we do make best shark fin soup, especially with fin of great white. This deadly beast so delicious; we love so much we cloned and bioengineered—much like your American chickens. These new Chinese Communist sharks are amazing, I must tell you. In just few short hours, these great whites reach full adult size, and can even survive in fresh water!"

The Chinese President paused for a moment before continuing.

"And yet," he continued, "I am not eating real shark fin soup tonight. The meat not meat, but tofu; we call it ToFin soup, is very good. You see, China has made deal with group you will soon label terrorists."

President Obama felt a chill run up his spine. Like most people, he already harbored an immense, natural fear of the great white shark, but being from Hawaii his own dread was especially acute. He had seen these sharks up close, had seen what they could do to people, and instead of desensitizing him to their presence in the ocean, it only made him fear them even worse.

Jinping's mere utterance of the term 'great white' was enough to make Obama shake with terror, but somehow he managed to steel himself before the Chinese President's watchful eyes.

"We are not here to talk about your bioengineered sharks, President Jinping," he said. "That is something you can discuss with the UN. What I want to know is, who are these terrorists you're working with? Is it Al-Qaeda? President Jinping, this would be a grave error if you have aligned yourself with terrorists; our countries may have great differences, but terrorists pose a threat to global stability!"

"President Obama," the Chinese President replied, "we are sick of global stability, don't you see? What we want is global dominance, much like you Americans have enjoyed in past century."

Obama was now officially losing his patience. "Who have you made a deal with?!" he shouted at the screen.

"You racistly assume Al-Qaeda," Jinping continued, "but conveniently forget about your own homegrown terrorists. Some of them even contributed to your first election campaign, but you have done nothing for them in return...."

"Who?!" demanded Senator Bernie Sanders.

"Yes, who?" Congresswoman Pelosi asked, more nicely.

The Chinese President ignored their impertinent questions. "These terrorists," he continued, "they reach out to us instead. They offer deal to help China, in exchange for switching to strictly vegan, cruelty-free diet. In fact, representatives from this group visited your White House, just earlier today...."

Senator Ted Cruz slammed his fist onto the table once again. "Son of bitch!" he screamed. "You mean to tell me that there's a vegan Al-Qaeda right here in America, and you have them visiting the White House, Mr. President?!"

Obama frowned disapprovingly at the insinuation. "No, Cruz," he replied, "I know exactly who he's talking about now, and I'm afraid it's not Al-Qaeda."

"WHO?!" all members of the CTF simultaneously demanded to know.

President Obama heaved a heavy sigh. "He's talking about PETA. I've always found their objectives to be somewhat... controversial... but, never treasonous or dangerous in any way.

As a matter of fact, they dropped by to discuss some pro-vegan policy proposals earlier today."

"Today?" gasped Senator Schumer.

"Oh no!" Michelle Bachmann piped up. "They could have left... Tofurkey products, or... bombs!"

The gathered politicians grew rapt at this revelation, dumbstruck by the potential security implications.

"Yes, they did visit," the Chinese President confirmed. "But do not worry. They did not leave bombs; they are not violent, this group PETA. They did leave something, however... perhaps some shark pheromones? Much like in film Snakes on Plane. Samuel L. Jackson is well-loved here in China, perhaps even more so than Yao Ming, but PETA... they have no love for you, America. They are, how you say in American, 'pissed-off' and very disappointed in your ignorance of animal rights."

John Boehner broke down and started to cry. "What... evil have these tofu-eating sons of bitches unleashed upon us?" he sobbed.

"Haha, tan man always cry," the Chinese President sneered. "Very funny on YouTube video. Your government weak, such weak fools, even from start. Your nation's founders so foolish to make capital on such low land. You Americans obsessed with oil, but you forget nature's first love—food. The world is one big food chain, and soon America will find itself below China on chain. The leaders of your worthless nation will make meager meal for our glorious great white sharks!"

"No!" Obama shouted, abandoning all pretense at playing cool. "You couldn't have!"

"Oh yes, we have. I'll have you know that PETA stocked our baby great whites in Potomac River shortly after meeting today.... You know, it would be shame if freak tsunami were to hit the Potomac tonight, especially with all this rain.... The sharks, you must realize, would have nowhere to go but inland. They'd be washed directly to you."

With that, the Chinese President took up his remote once again. Lightning struck at the click of a button, and the rain began falling even harder than ever on Washington, D.C. An ominous rumble could be heard coming from the southeast, and the ground began to shake.

"Your pathetic home," Jinping concluded, "is sure to be a Great White House tonight...."

Chapter 3

The tsunami hit them hard and fast, a bit like those selfies Congressman Weiner used to enjoy sharing with his colleagues and constituents before being forced to resign.

Gathered by the south-facing window in the East Room, the politicians could only look on in horror as a dark wall of water rose up before them, carrying cars, billboards, half of the Washington Monument, and the entire contents of the Potomac River along with it.

Seconds later, the massive wave broke against the White House, doing great structural damage to the building and triggering its automated defenses. The East Room itself was flooded knee deep in water as the windows imploded, pelting the CTF with shards of glass and scattering them like a spooked school of fish.

A group of Secret Service agents burst in with guns drawn, wading into the morass of broken furniture and half-drowned politicians.

"We must leave now, Mr. President!" barked Head Agent Cardinal, grabbing Obama by the back of his suit coat as he tried to fish him up.

"No, Birdman!" Obama coughed, sloshing to his feet. The agent had earned this nickname through his resemblance to the Miami Heat basketball player. "I must... reason with the Chinese President...."

Wedged against the room's north wall, the communications console had miraculously remained intact. As President Obama lurched his way toward it, the image of President Jinping once again appeared upon its cracked, diagonally skewed screen. Casually calling his cat back into his lap, he acted as if he hadn't just launched a massive, weather-based attack against the most powerful nation in the world.

To say that Obama was angry and upset would have been an understatement, but he did his best to remain calm. "President Jinping," he began, "you've shown us your new weapon. We respect its power, but we must act reasonably here and we must stay focused on the issue at hand: our debt. You must not do another weather attack!"

"President Obama," the Chinese leader sighed, "I am reasonable. I swear this only time I use our country's weather weapon, just like your own country only use nuclear bomb one time on Japan."

President Obama was left speechless by the comparison.

"Okay, so two times you use bomb. It no matter. Now you know we mean business. We just want our money, Mr. President, but PETA... they want revenge for what you do to those poor American animals. They want you to know what it like to be hunted."

"Hunted?"

"Yes, hunted. If you look outside right now, you might get picture...."

Splashing his way back over to the south side of the room,

passing the floundering members of the CTF along the way, President Obama stood before the broken windows and gazed out into the eerie, sudden stillness of the night. Though pockets of lightning still flashed in the distance, the rain had died down considerably for the moment, and the moon had finally begun to show itself through the storm clouds high above.

Having risen past the ground floor, the flood waters lapped lazily against the state floor as though it were a fishing dock. Obama was astounded that the White House hadn't been washed away completely, but he was even more amazed by how calm things seemed in comparison to only minutes before.

That's when he noticed the dark triangular shapes, slicing like sailboats across the water's moonlit surface.

Shark fins.

"OH, SNAP!!!" Obama screamed, spinning back around to face Jinping. "I should have listened to Huntsman... you Chinese... you're mad!"

"Yes, we are mad," the Chinese President echoed from across the room. "We get mad when money owed us, when deadbeats no pay up. Huntsman did know our tricks, this is true, but it no matter now. Mark my words, Mr. President—your White House will be Red House tonight, unless you pay your debt. We know how to stop sharks; we have ways if you pay right now, or else..."

"Or else WHAT?!" bellowed Vice President Biden, drunkenly staggering to Obama's side.

"...you and your government leaders will be shark fin soup by sunrise. We shall speak again when you come to your senses, and are ready to pay debt. Bai bai...."

With that, the screen went black.

By now, most of the CTF had recovered from the deluge, but they remained in a state of collective shock. Stumbling around with her tangled hair and torn-up dress, Congresswoman Bachmann looked like she had just been raped by a pack of wild welfare abusers.

"Well," said Ted Cruz, swimming out from underneath a table, "I'll be damned, Obama. We got ourselves some Communist sharks on the loose. Good thing I got my gun with me! Second Amendment ain't so stupid now, huh?" Standing up, he drew a revolver with a Texas flag emblazoned on its butt from his jacket. "Just point me at those sons of bitches, and I'll teach them the meaning of 'stand your ground'."

Obama wasn't quite sure how to address Cruz's proposal in a politically sensitive manner, but an angry, drunk Joe Biden apparently wasn't holding the same reservations.

"I don't believe this B.S.!" he yelled to no one in particular. "The Chinese, they have holograms! It's Chinaman tricks, I tell you—Tupac stuff. They did a video game thing... but they can't control the weather!"

"Now, Joe," Obama cautioned, but there was just no reaching the man.

"That's ridiculous!" the Vice President continued with his rant. "Uncle Joe is no fool, and he knows this is a bunch of malarkey. Here, I'll even show ya!"

Without hesitation, Vice President Biden marched over to the nearest window, sticking his head out between the broken panes. "Ooooooooh," he said with mock fear. "Shark fins, fake water. I tell ya boys, I ain't fallin'—"

Before he could even finish his sentence, a great white leapt up and snapped its jaws around his neck, taking his head clean off as it splashed back into the water.

"They got Joe!" Speaker Boehner sobbed, startling Congresswoman Pelosi with a sudden embrace from behind. "I hated that son of a bitch, but those commie sharks got Biden!"

Meanwhile, the Vice President's headless body teetered on the windowsill, about to fall out after it.

"No!" cried Paul Ryan, lunging for the bloody corpse of his departed friend. Maybe it was just the booze talking, but somehow he felt confident he could use his P90X strength to save Biden's remains from the Communist sharks.

"Get away from that window, Paul!" Obama cried out.

But it was too late. Just as Senator Ryan got ahold of Biden, another great white emerged, shearing off the arms of the man who once wrote a bill aimed at getting America out of debt. The irony was not lost on Ryan as he dropped to his knees, arm stumps spurting blood and bone marrow to either side.

Before anyone could get any dumb ideas about trying to save him, a shark rammed itself into the White House at top speed, lodging its body in the window frame. Locking four rows of razor-sharp teeth around the doomed Senator's torso, the twenty-four-foot beast tore him to shreds right in front of them like a great white garbage disposal.

The shark remained stuck in the window even after it had finished its snack, chomping the air and thrashing about for more politicians to fill its bloody maw. The Secret Service agents opened fire, aiming for its eyes and mouth, but still it swung its head around, ravenous for more red or blue meat. When the swing shark finally dislodged itself, it took the window frame right along with it as it swam back into the depths.

Agent Birdman had finally seen enough. "Everyone this way!" he ordered. "We're heading to the JFK tunnel."

"Wait!" cried Senator Sanders, as the others rushed for the door.

"Wait for what?" asked Senator McCaskill.

"Where's Ted?"

The group looked around the room and at each other. There was some general shrugging of shoulders.

"Uhhh, guys," said Senator Cruz, swimming back out from his hiding spot under the table. "I'm right here...."

"Where were you during the firefight, John Wayne?" asked Congresswoman Pelosi. "These brave boys could've used your help against that shark, you know." As she said this, she winked at one Secret Service agent and pinched another on the ass.

"Yeah, yeah...." was all he could say for himself.

Agent Birdman marched up to Cruz as he crawled to his feet and pistol whipped him right in the face.

"Owww!" cried Cruz, rubbing the deep red welt on his cheek. "Whadya do that for?"

Agent Birdman grabbed him by the collar and pulled him in close. "You're holding up the group," he said matter-of-factly. "That happens again, I swear to fucking god I'll fucking feed you to those motherfucking sharks myself. Do I make myself clear?"

Cruz nodded emphatically and Birdman let him go.

"Now c'mon, folks; follow me this way!"

Traversing the state floor of the White House, the group sloshed through some areas less flooded than others, but there was no denying that quite a bit of water had permeated the presidential residence already. Groping along as they followed the dim emergency lights, Congresswoman Bachmann was surprised that none of the liberals present tried groping her in the dark as well.

The tunnels had been a tough decision on Birdman's part. While the upper floors would've been the more obvious choice, there was just no telling when another wave might hit, or how high the waters would ultimately rise. Given the airtight structure of the JFK tunnel, he'd decided that this was probably their safest bet for now.

Years ago, on his training for the job, Birdman had learned that the tunnels were made from the same kind of metal forming Wolverine's skeleton and claws—adamantium. The tunnel, though underground, eventually led to a helipad on the surface where JFK would often meet his mistresses. Helicopters made the arrivals seem much more official, thus raising fewer questions from Jackie and the press.

Usually when Obama and Birdman visited the tunnels together, they joked about finding strands of Marilyn Monroe's pubic hair down there. Tonight though, the Chinese Communist shark attack had muted all possible humor on the subject.

At the state floor landing, the beleaguered politicians were relieved to find that the ground floor wasn't entirely underwater. Luckily, the automated shutters had done their job, preventing a full-scale inundation of the lower levels. Swiftly they made their way down the grand staircase, shivering in soaking wet clothes as they followed Birdman and Obama.

Reaching the library, Agent Birdman took a quick headcount while President Obama punched his secret code into a wall panel behind the portrait of Buddy and Socks, the Clinton's old dog and cat. Obama often wondered why they'd kept the painting up, not to mention why the Bush's left it up during their own tenure in the White House, but this was no time to be pondering such matters.

A nearby bookshelf slid over to one side, revealing a hidden passageway. Obama nodded to Birdman who led the way, the other Secret Service men herding the rest of the politicians underground.

When they arrived at the entrance to the tunnel itself, the agents examined the area for any signs of water, but there was not a drop to be found in the vicinity. They conveniently ignored a few half-empty Gatorade and vodka bottles strewn about, leftovers from some tough days Obama faced while pushing through his healthcare bill.

As the tunnel's entrance ground open to admit them, the group sighed with collective relief upon witnessing the first dry space they'd seen since the attack.

Obama had been anticipating it, so he wasn't too surprised by Senator Sanders' initial reaction to the vastness of the tunnel. "I can't believe this, President Obama," the Independent Socialist said. "Do you have any idea how many homeless people there are in D.C.? This space could be used to house them."

Ignoring his comments, the party pushed forward, powered

along by a deep sense of guilt.

"Well, it's true..." Sander's muttered from the back. "Jeez!"

They walked along in silence after that, but it wasn't long before Birdman came to an abrupt halt, raising a fist to stop the others.

"Do you hear that?" he said, cocking an ear forward.

"Hear what?" asked Senator Harry Reid.

"It sounds like... hard to say. Could be... flowing water up ahead...."

"You have got to be kidding me..." groaned former Secretary of the Treasury Timothy Geithner.

"Maybe it's just wind?" opined Federal Reserve Chairman Ben Bernanke.

Senator Rand Paul looked upon the economist with disdain. "Since when has wind ever sounded like water?"

The politicians resumed their usual bickering until Agent Birdman turned around and told them all something very similar to what he'd singled out Cruz for earlier.

"...and I am not playing this time, got it?"

"Bu-but Birdman..." Senator Schumer objected meekly.

The agent was in his face before he could say another word. "What did I just tell you, punk?"

"Umm, Mr. Birdman?" Senator Rubio thought to interject, eyes growing wide as he pointed to something behind the agent.

"Motherfucker!" Birdman yelled. "What is it?"

He didn't have to read more than two or three faces before turning back around to see what they were all staring at.

"Run!" Birdman screamed, his brown face suddenly turning white. "Head back! Now!"

Up ahead, where the passage curved out of sight, a small stream of water had clearly begun flowing into the tunnel. The trickle soon became a torrent, and moments later there were thousands of gallons of water gushing after the fleeing group.

This would've been bad enough had it not been for the five

or six sharks, riding the wave like muscular surfboards of death.

"God damn you, Clinton!" Obama huffed as he ran. "You just had to build your own entrance, didn't you?"

"What are you talking about?" yelled Senator McCain, running surprising fast for such an old guy.

"Let's just say that JFK wasn't the only hound dog who used this tunnel as his own underground poon train!" Obama yelled back in response. "His tampering with the original construction must've weakened its integrity!"

"Let's GO, people!" Birdman hollered, glancing back at the rapidly approaching shark wave. "Hurry!"

At his order, two junior agents broke off from the rest of the group, staying behind with their pistols ready. Like pawns on a chessboard, they waited until the sharks came within range before opening fire.

It's hard to say how effective their gambit proved to be. The two sharks in the lead turned the youngest agent into a human wishbone, splitting him apart at the legs. The other agent was swallowed almost entirely whole by another shark, snipping him off at his feet before he'd even run out of bullets.

Most of the politicians made it back to the tunnel's entrance with plenty of time to spare, but Congressman Tim Scott was lagging behind. "Wait for me!" he screamed.

"We can't leave Tim!" yelled the President as he was wrestled through the tunnel's exit.

"We have to close this door!" Birdman screamed in his ear.

The poor guy never stood a chance.

Though a Tea Partier, Tim Scott typically stayed away from water; he swam quite poorly and could barely even float. Bobbing up and down like a raspberry tea bag, each time he emerged from the rolling torrent the water was left redder than before. And the redder it became, the hungrier those sharks got.

Safely ensconced behind the tunnel door, no one even heard the Congressman's final garbled screams.

Chapter 4

There was not much time for mourning, however. Preoccupied more with their own survival than anything else, the remaining CTF members followed the Secret Service team back upstairs, retreating to the relative safety of the State Dining Room.

Within the space of half an hour, three of them had already been lost to the Communist sharks, their legacies and politics quickly forgotten. Those left breathing had only one item left on their agendas—living through the night.

"How do we get through this, Birdie?" Obama asked his head agent. "They got Joe, and even though I personally could've done without the other two, they were still good men. Men who only wanted the best for their country. And your boys, Diego and Tom.... We simply can't afford to lose any more people here tonight." Obama paused to reflect on their predicament. "What are we going to do?"

Birdman wondered if his Commander in Chief could see

into his eyes, how lost he looked behind his dark sunglasses. For his special assignments training, he'd gone through so many hypothetical scenarios, including one on shark attacks, but that had been in preparation for the Obamas' visit to SeaWorld, not some unthinkable White House ambush. There was just no protocol for this type of situation.

Still, he had one job to do—protect the man he'd come to love as a brother, and if he could, the rest of the CTF as well.

Birdman considered the President's words, but there was no time to mourn their losses or even plan their next move. There was only time to go with his gut and do his best to make sure Obama didn't end up in the gut of a shark.

"We're safe here for now," he said, adjusting his earpiece, "but if this rain doesn't let up, the waters will only rise.... I'm going to call headquarters, see if I can—"

Obama placed a reassuring hand on the agent's muscular shoulder. "Birdie, I have full confidence in your ability to lead us out of this mess. You have my trust." Looking out amongst his enemies and allies alike, he continued, "Let's just remain calm, people."

Speaking into his lapel clip, Birdman proceeded to contact Homeland Security.

"This is Agent Birdman," he reported in. "The President is safe, but... and I say this in all seriousness, there are sharks surrounding the White House. Yes, I said sharks. Real motherfucking sharks. The water is rising in D.C., and our group has sustained several casualties already."

Birdman paused here, listening through the static for a response.

"We need to get the hell out of here," he continued. "We need an emergency evac, now! Send boats, helicopters, whatever you've got to send."

"What are they saying?" inquired Bernie Sanders.

"Are you getting through?" John Boehner asked with a

sniffle.

Ignoring them, Birdman continued listening intently to his radio. "Mayday, Mayday... do you copy? Shit!"

In a moment of frustration, Birdman plucked out his earpiece and threw it across the room.

Going to collect it, President Obama picked it up and walked back over to where the distressed agent had slumped against the wall, slowly sinking to the floor.

"Don't you flake out on us, Birdie," he said, crouching down to hand him back his earpiece. "Not now. The American government is depending on you."

"We want to know what HLS had to say!" demanded Harry Reid.

"Yes," seconded Eric Cantor, "please, Agent Birdman!"

"I... I couldn't make it out," he stammered in response, lifting his head from where it rested in his arms. "Lost the damn signal...."

Lightning struck as the storm seemed to worsen, and grim looks were exchanged around the room. The deep, booming thunder sounded like a death knell to many in the group.

"Hey!" Senator McCain blurted out, suddenly leaping from his chair. "I think I hear something!"

"What is it, John?" urged President Obama.

"I think it's a chopper, maybe several," he replied, "getting close!"

Rushing over to the windows, the group of them jostled for a look outside.

Sure enough, in the distance there were two Black Hawk helicopters, ostensibly heading their way. The entire CTF erupted into spontaneous jubilation at the mere sight of them, hugging each other and hopping up and down in a display they hoped their voters would never see.

"We're saved!" squealed former Secretary of the Treasury Timothy Geithner.

"It's a miracle!" cried Senator Rubio.

"Wait..." said Agent Birdman, breaking up their reverie just as abruptly as they'd started it. "Something's wrong!"

There were several deep gasps as they turned to confirm his statement. One of the choppers was clearly struggling to stay in flight, buffeted by rising winds on its approach. Bobbing and weaving through the air, several of its crew were flung from the gunship, dropping like bait into the water. Before they even hit its surface, ravenous sharks leapt up to snap them out of midair.

"Oh my God!" cried Congresswoman Bachmann.

"No, no, no!" yelled Senator Cruz.

A lightning bolt lit up the sky, blinding them momentarily, but when their vision returned their worst fears were confirmed: The second Black Hawk had been hit. Trailing smoke as it lost altitude, its spinning blades clipped the other chopper before a giant great white emerged right beneath it. Latching on with its powerful jaws, the leviathan brought the gunship down as though it were a toy.

Meanwhile, the other chopper was coming in hot.

"Hit the deck!" screamed Agent Birdman, just before it crashed into the South Portico.

The entire building shook with violent force as the Black Hawk exploded in a ball of flame, and those who hadn't already gotten down on their own volition were instantly knocked to the floor.

One by one, the members of the CTF slowly rose to their feet, dusting themselves off as the stench of smoke and burning fuel filled the air.

"Well, what now?" coughed Congresswoman Pelosi, straightening her hair.

"We are truly, deeply fucked..." muttered Senator Paul.

Obama, though a true liberal at heart, did not hold much faith in the Federal Government either. Especially not in this situation. It was at that moment he finally realized they were on their own; they'd have to be willing to act independently if they expected to prevail against the sharks.

Some of his critics considered him too professorial, too cool to inspire much camaraderie in his followers, but deep down he knew he was a leader; he had proven as much back in college, when he scored the best marijuana for a campus party and even brought together the chess and basketball teams, who were often competing for the same girls.

If nothing else, Obama had faith in himself, and he knew that he could lead them out of this mess. All he had to do was look at the problem logically. Bin Laden, the Tea Party, and even sharks were all just problems with logical solutions, but the real problem facing them tonight was time, and it definitely wasn't on their side.

If they didn't find some way out of there, and soon, Obama was certain that the sharks would devour every last one of them. That's what they'd been bioengineered to do, and that's what President Jinping would use his weather control powers to ensure. Still, what they needed now was information; they simply didn't have enough data to make an informed decision on anything yet.

"Everyone, follow me," President Obama finally said, addressing his colleagues. "There's a TV in the Green Room, powered by the emergency generators. I know it will work; I couldn't miss SportsCenter after all, not after the great blizzard of 2010. At any rate, we need to see what the media's reporting on the outside world. We'll need that info before we can decide where we're going and how we are going to get there."

Ben Bernanke and Timothy Geithner exchanged a glance, both of them shrugging apathetically. They couldn't predict the financial crisis of 2008, and so they didn't feel especially confident making this call either.

The Republicans all looked to their leaders, McCain and Boehner, who begrudgingly nodded in agreement with the

Commander in Chief.

"Maybe we'll hear of some other rescues," Boehner suggested.

It was decided.

Making their way down the hall, the remaining CTF members all grabbed seats in the Green Room. Some of them were forced to stand due to a lack of chairs, but some of them were willing to double up on each other's laps. No one was surprised when Senators Rubio and Schumer wound up sharing a seat together, as the two of them had recently worked quite closely on an anti-immigration bill.

Once everyone had settled in, Obama took up the remote and put on his favorite cable news channel, MSNBC. The conservatives in the group all groaned at the sight of Chris Matthews' pale yet ruddy face, hovering over a headline that read, WASHINGTON, D.C. TSUNAMI: WHITE HOUSE DOWN.

"We've just learned that there has been a freak tsunami in Washington tonight," Matthews was in the middle of saying. "We have received confirmation that President Obama is safe, but Vice President Biden, a true American hero of the working class and poor, a man who took the train to work every day, has been killed."

"How does he know that part?" Obama asked, looking around the room. "We've got more than just water leaks in the White House, apparently."

A few of the agents and politicians discreetly pocketed their phones, hoping that he hadn't noticed their tweeting.

"There are even rumors of sharks coming inland with the floodwaters," Matthews continued. "These sharks have allegedly surrounded the White House, which remains under a cloud of especially bad weather tonight. We don't have all the details, but one thing I can say for sure is that this is clearly a result of global warming."

At this remark, Senator Cruz took off his shoe and threw it at the TV, just barely missing its screen. "I don't care how much of a boner he gets listening to you speak, President Obama," he said. "That guy's a moron. Put on Fox, maybe they'll have some actual news for us."

"All right, Senator Cruz," Obama said, "fair enough." He picked up the remote and switched the station, much to the chagrin of the liberals present.

Meanwhile, over on Fox, there was Brit Hume's face above a similar headline. WASHINGTON, D.C. TSUNAMI: WHITE HOUSE DROWN, it read.

"As strange as it sounds," Hume began, "our sources claim that PETA has unleashed sharks upon the capitol. It's likely they are working with Jihadist scientists, who are perhaps even manipulating the weather. We don't know how Al-Qaeda is behind this, but we're pretty sure they are. It makes sense that Islamic radicals and PETA would join forces, after all—in fact, it was really only a matter of time, as both groups are united in their unwillingness to eat pork. As for the President, he is reportedly safe, but due to freak lightning, winds, and ongoing flooding in the area, all rescue efforts have been thwarted thus far. We can only hope and pray that the President and Congress make it out of this predicament alive."

Hume paused then, touching his earpiece. "We've just received word that two truly great men, Paul Ryan and Tim Scott, have been taken from us. Sources, ummm, followers of McCain's Twitter feed have reported that they were both eaten alive by PETA sharks."

Obama shot McCain a disapproving look.

"I don't know," Hume continued, "just speaking off the cuff here... maybe it's just me, but when you don't eat meat, perhaps you get a little crazy in the head? But for now though, let us have a moment of silence for these two American heroes. They have fallen and will be missed... oh yeah, and by the way, Vice

President Biden has also reportedly been killed."

Obama shook his head in anger and switched the channel to CNN. "It has been confirmed that a new species of shark has attacked the White House," Wolf Blitzer was saying, "and that one of them has eaten our Vice President, Joe Biden. Senators Paul Ryan and Tim Scott were also reportedly consumed. The Navy is currently recovering from the freak weather surge in Washington tonight, with auxiliary ships trying to reach the White House as we speak."

Some members of the CTF appeared hopeful at this prospect, others quite skeptical.

"Multiple vessels have already been lost in the ongoing rescue efforts, with the heart of the storm inexplicably centered directly over the White House itself. All citizens are advised to evacuate the area immediately. Also, please do not try swimming with the sharks; they are dangerous. Right now, all we can do is keep the President in our prayers. Obviously, this is a sign of the dangers of global warming, and maybe even oceanic mercury levels affecting natural shark behavior. We can't be sure."

Switching back over MSNBC, they caught Chris Matthews saying "...only moments ago, the Chinese government released an official statement pledging aid to our nation in its time of need."

"They really are conniving bastards," Obama sighed, finally shutting off the TV. "Hell, they'll probably just tack their 'aid' onto our debt...."

"So, the media is basically useless," said Senator Rubio. "What do we do now?"

"Well, we can't just wait around," Obama replied. "Based on what we've seen and what we've learned here tonight, President Jinping will do everything in his power to keep us isolated and helpless; we'll have to find a solution for ourselves. I'm open to suggestions."

It was then that Nancy Pelosi sensed her chance to be useful.

"The rapper LL Cool J, who supported my campaign, was once in a movie about sharks," she said. "But, he was only able to save himself by stabbing one in the eye with a crucifix."

Congresswoman Bachmann nodded. "The she-devil has a point. We all need to pray like Mr. Cool J did and use the power of Jesus Christ to save us."

President Obama was not pleased at all with these nonconstructive solutions.

"Congresswoman Bachmann," he said, "while I respect and share your faith, like the old proverb goes, we can't wait for God to save us from drowning when there's a boat right around the corner. What is our boat? How can we escape these sharks? The water is rising. What we need now are practical solutions."

Nancy Pelosi grinned so wide then, the others could almost see her elation through the Botox.

"There has always been a solution for every problem facing America," she said. "And that solution is solar power."

Chapter 5

Nancy Pelosi was often hated and sometimes naive, but she was not stupid. Like her creative daughter, who had risen to the top of documentary filmmaking, the Italian-American Congresswoman understood one thing—ideas were power, and she had one to help stop the Communist sharks.

The idea originated from the time she took her daughter to see Jaws 2 (a lesser film than the original), which involved the use of electricity as a weapon. The way she figured, if they could somehow trick the sharks into attacking the solar array on the White House roof, they could electrocute them to death just like in the movie.

The only question was—who would carry out the Pelosi Plan?

Like any important vote to come before Congress, the bill was passed with an amendment that she would have to carry it out herself. It was agreed that this was clearly a two-person job, however, and so the conservatives drew straws to see who would assist. Senator Cruz was the loser, but he still felt like a winner anyway, because now he'd finally have the chance redeem himself. He was determined to stand his ground against those sharks.

"Look, Birdie," President Obama said, addressing the head agent, "you stay here. Send a few of your men with Congresswoman Pelosi and Senator Cruz to the roof. The solar panels absorbed a great deal of energy before the storm today, so the batteries should be fully charged. As Congresswoman Pelosi said, if they can trick the sharks into attacking these panels, hopefully the charge will be enough to cause a mass electrocution. I'm afraid this is the best solution we have for now."

Scientifically, the plan wasn't very sound at all, but it was a fact of life in Washington that it's better to try fixing problems even when there's no obvious solution. Minority Leader Pelosi happened to be a fan of that philosophy herself.

"Thank you, Mr. President," she said with a salute. "I believe this plan can work. It will prove the effectiveness of solar power while at the same time saving us all. Come on, Senator Cruz," she continued. "We've got some sharks to kill...."

Cruz nodded, twirling his gun on his finger as he followed her out the door. Two Secret Service men accompanied them, pistols drawn and ready for action.

It was still raining quite heavily when they reached the roof. Lightning flashed uncomfortably close nearby. Still, Pelosi believed in her plan, and she was determined to implement it regardless of weather.

Together she and Senator Cruz braced themselves against the gusting winds, fighting their way over to the solar panels President Obama had recently installed. Looking down over the edge of the roof, they kept a close eye on the sharks slowly circling the White House.

"You don't think they can jump this high, do you?" asked Senator Cruz.

"Nah," Congresswoman Pelosi replied, shielding her eyes against the rain. "They're sharks, not flying fish, you moron."

"But how are we going to get them to attack way up here? This isn't more of your usual liberal nonsense, Pelosi, now is it?"

Reaching the solar array, she turned to Cruz with a mischievous smile on her face. "I thought you'd never ask…" she said. "Here, give me your hand."

"What? Why?" he asked, pulling it away as she drew her knife.

"Sharks are attracted to blood, Senator Cruz. I am going to cut your hand so you can smear your blood all over these solar panels."

"You're out of you goddamned mind!" he cried. "Besides, I get really squeamish at the sight of blood. Can't we just, you know… use some of your… period blood instead?"

"Sir!" came her stern reply, slapping him hard across the face. "I'll have you know that I am a 72-year-old woman. Did you not reap the benefits of public school sex education as a young man? Now here," she said, grabbing his hand before he could pull away again. "This will only hurt a bit…."

Senator Cruz screamed high and loud, almost like a little girl, as Congresswoman Pelosi made a small incision in his left palm. Still, he did as he was told, dutifully smearing his blood over several of the solar panels.

Completing this task, Cruz fell back to stand watch with his gun drawn, looking on as Pelosi and one of the Secret Service agents lifted a solar panel between them. It turned out to be much heavier than she'd expected, but she dug in deep, strengthened and inspired by all the underpaid women in the world. With much effort, they successfully wrangled it over to the edge of the roof.

"This is it!" she cried, turning to face the men present. "I, Nancy Pelosi, will finally demonstrate the value of solar power, proving the worth of women in government once and for all!"

With a deep grunt, she then attempted to push the panel off the roof, but unfortunately she pushed a little too hard. Slipping in the puddle beneath her feet, she fell headfirst after the alternative energy device, splashing down beside it as it sank into the shark-infested waters.

Hanging onto the panel like a shield, the mighty San Franciscan used it to deflect the charge of a twenty-six-foot great white, which very nearly knocked it right out of her frail, old hands. Still, she knew she wouldn't last long against the beasts now surrounding her.

Accepting her fate as shark food, her only dying wish was to perish by electrocution before the great whites devoured her. When the next shark came lunging in, she saw her opportunity and took it.

Mustering up her last ounce of strength, Pelosi rammed that solar panel straight down its gullet.

She expected to feel a shock, or at least some kind of tingling sensation, as the great white crushed the panel in its jaws. She expected to feel the warmth and serenity of Heaven, basking in its light as the angels came down to take her. She expected to be lit up like a roman candle on the Fourth of July, if nothing else, but...

...it didn't work. No sparks, no electricity—just shattered glass that sliced her arms, spilling even more blood into the water.

In that moment, it finally occurred to her that the battery might have made a better choice than the solar panel.

Petrified, Pelosi screamed out something she never thought in a million years she'd say:

"Shoot, Senator Cruz! Now!"

The men up top opened fire, hammering the sharks with a hail of bullets. Cruz even managed to belt out a manly-sounding battle cry as he emptied his revolver into the monsters.

But it was all for naught; they had Pelosi surrounded,

and they gobbled her up like a sausage in her grandmother's homemade spaghetti sauce.

Before they could even register the failure of her plan, their thoughts were interrupted by a deafening boom and a blinding flash of lightning, striking one of the Secret Service men dead where he stood. His fried black body toppled over, knocking both himself and his partner down into the bloody stew below.

Performing a hasty sign of the cross, Cruz hightailed it out of there, not wanting to be struck by any Chinese 'Satan-Pagan-God-Zeus' lightning himself.

"Stupid solar panels!" he spat, barging back into the Green Room. "The plan didn't work, and now Pelosi is just some Italian meatball in a shark's stomach, same with your boys. So, what do we do now? These sharks are no joke, I tell ya, they're more dangerous than the Mexicans and the terrorists combined!"

Michele Bachmann nodded sadly, like it came as no surprise. "God rest that godless soul of hers," she said. "We should have prayed." Clasping her hands and lowering her head, she added, "I'm starting with or without the rest of you."

Meanwhile, everyone else in the room looked to President Obama for the answer.

"Look," he said, "I see no other choice. We must negotiate with China. I can stop this madness before more lives are lost. I can make them see the error of their ways. I ran as a diplomat, and by God, I'm going to show that I can talk some sense into even the maddest of madmen."

The CTF certainly had their reservations about this, but they didn't try stopping him as he went over to the TV, motioning for Birdman to help him set up another comm link. Obama didn't care what anyone else thought; he was ready to bring his best diplomacy game.

Chapter 6

The second conference call with China was set up like a movie theater, with those who had the most political power sitting closest to the screen. As the static began to dissipate, the Chinese President appeared in a golden jumpsuit this time, benching weights with two beefy-looking bodyguards spotting him. He finished several more reps before finally cradling the bar and sitting up, panting with exertion as he prepared to address the group.

"Oh, Hello President Obama," he began, casually toweling off his brow. "I have been watching the news; terrible what is happening with weather.... Most channels are blaming global warming." Jinping paused here to survey the group onscreen. "Oh, dear.... I see some of you have gone missing. Where is Biden, and math-boy Paul Ryan? What a shame if shark ate them up.... Though I see Bernanke still alive," he continued. "He will make shark very full. Hahaha, he so fat!"

Bernanke became a little self-conscious at Jinping's obvious remark, but he didn't say anything in his defense.

President Obama felt a deep anger welling up inside of him. The last time he had felt like this was when he was a kid, back on the ball courts of Hawaii, going head to head with the much bigger, stronger Polynesians who always treated him like an outsider.

"We have lost a few of our number," he confirmed. "They are dead, sir. You've killed many good men and one great woman already tonight. They all died horrible deaths."

"I did no such thing, President Obama. PETA unleashed the sharks, may I remind you. We just wanted give them good home, being animal-loving vegans as we are now. Looks like world agrees with that story, too! Media in every country so predictable...."

President Obama looked back at his colleagues, most of whom remained timid in the Chinese leader's presence. Senator Cruz was the only one with enough balls to speak up.

"We oughta nuke you fried rice-eating bastards!" he spat.

For a moment, Obama actually found himself considering that a nuclear attack might be their best option at this point, sighing heavily at the gravity of the situation.

"Senator Cruz," he said, "we are not launching any nukes here tonight. Justified or not, it will seem like an unprovoked attack. We cannot start World War III over this. We have to be better than that; we have to remain reasonable."

"You are reasonable man," Jinping said, "but it is your pocketbook that has unleashed these sharks, you see. Your continual spending and failure to pay debts have left us no choice but to send these... loan sharks. Hahaha, I so funny! But we can still stop them if you pay us money now. You pay now, Mr. Obama, and we make sharks go away!"

"But how can you honestly expect us to come up with a trillion dollars overnight?" asked President Obama. "We'd have to slash what little's left of our nation's social safety net."

"No, Mr. President!" shouted Senator Sanders. "I'd rather be thrown to the sharks myself than see any further cuts to Social Security and Medicare. It will be damn-near impossible to pay this debt without cutting nearly all social services, and you know it! And you, Mr. Jinping," he continued, shaking an admonishing finger at the camera, "you are not a real Communist; you are nothing but a capitalist vegan piece of scum!"

President Obama felt like he was stuck between two warring factions, much like speaking before Congress, only with much higher stakes.

"That's enough, Senator Sanders," he said, returning his attention to the Chinese leader. "President Jinping, this must end now. Surely you must see that this is pure madness."

"No!" countered Jinping. "This! Is! CHINA!!! I always wanted say that, hahaha.... We love your American movies so much, you know. So no. You no pay debt, we no stop sharks."

President Obama had finally had enough. "Birdman," he said, "shut this TV off. I can't stand to look at this tyrant any longer. President Bush was right—there really are true evildoers in this world."

The Chinese President waved cheerily goodbye as Birdman deactivated the comm link as ordered. An uneasy silence fell upon the room, and the CTF remained speechless for some time after that, which only made the rain and the thunder and the howling winds seem even louder.

The water would continue to rise.

And the sharks were getting closer.

Obama felt more anger than fear in his heart, and he found himself quite tempted to bum a smoke from Boehner. Anything to help calm his frazzled nerves. Completely out of character for a man not known for showing his emotions, Obama abruptly got up, walked across the room, and punched a hole in the wall.

"I feel your anger, President Obama," said Senator Rand Paul, slowly sauntering over to him, "but I have a constructive solution I'd like to offer."

"All right, Senator Paul," Obama replied, wringing his smarting hand. "Let's hear it. A solution is what we desperately need here tonight."

"Okay," Paul began. "Very simple: we abolish the Federal Government and sell off all its assets. This would net us enough cash to pay off the Chinese and everyone else we owe money to as well. I mean, besides the army, why do we even really need a Federal Government? God might be using these sharks as a sign, a sign showing us the way to a truly free, market-driven country. Who is John Galt?" he asked by way of conclusion. "A man who wants to stop these sharks."

Obama regarded the senator with the same quiet intensity he'd showed Hilary in the primaries.

"Senator Paul," he said, "with all due respect, please shut your goddamned mouth. You know we can't do that. And besides, the only country that could probably afford to buy us out in the first place is China. Congressman Boehner," he continued, looking over to John in the corner, "stop crying and give me a cigarette. I need a smoke and we need to talk. You too, Birdman."

"Okay, fine," Senator Paul responded. "You two smoke your death sticks, but it's our debt that's going to get us all killed here tonight."

President Obama ignored him. He never liked the man and he didn't trust people who wore toupees in general; they were usually the ones full of the most crazy-ass ideas. Taking a cigarette from Boehner, he lit up and took a deep drag.

"We've got to find some way out of here," he said, exhaling a thick plume of smoke. "Things will only get worse until we do."

"Are you sure you don't want to try Paul's idea?" Speaker Boehner said, wiping tears from his face. "Maybe we could use his offer as part of some grand bargain."

"Let me be clear, John," Obama replied, "I am not going to

let our policies be dictated by bullies and terrorists. Right now we must protect the American people."

"Cut the crap, Barack," countered Boehner. "You're smoking a cigarette, not a Hawaii Five-O, or whatever hip term you use for marijuana. Don't give me these platitudes and bullshit about the American people."

"No, John, I'm being serious. As serious as your perpetual sunburn. Listen... I know of a group of scientists here in Washington. Kerry knows them, too. They're all geniuses, and experts on weather patterns to boot. If we can reach them and bring them here, I believe they can help us find a solution."

"Kerry? That dumb son of a bitch went out yachting just before the storm. He's probably dead by now, too.... Sorry, but who are these scientists again?"

"They're actually a group from meetup.com," Obama replied. "Scientists With Swag, or SWS they call themselves. It's a silly name, I'll admit. I imagine they don't do too well with the ladies either, but from what I hear, these are brilliant men. They even build their own drones in their free time, flying them for fun. I told the CIA to leave them alone, in case we ever needed to call upon them in an emergency. It was a good decision, looking back on it. And apparently they're holding a meeting tonight, right up at Ben's Chili's Bowl. They are scientists and chili enthusiasts."

Boehner nodded his head reluctantly. "They do have good chili there..." he said. "Well, hell. I'm all out of ideas. If these nerds can help us, I say let's take it. We need all the help we can get here, right guys? What about you, Birdman?" he continued, "What's the latest on our rescue?"

"Still got nothing," he said. "Assuming the Navy gets their shit together, who knows if they'll even succeed in getting a boat through to us. They already tried helicopters, and thanks to Senator Paul's filibuster on drone policy, those are probably out, too."

Senator Paul resented the agent's statement, but deep down

he knew that he was at least partially to blame for their lack of drone options.

"And even if we could find some drones to lay a smackdown on these sharks," Birdman continued, "who knows if they'd even be able to fly in this weather? Hell, you saw what happened out there—seems anything gets close to us, it misfires and goes down."

"Damn it..." Obama sighed. "I knew I should have stuck to my guns on those drones."

"Honestly," Birdman said, "if you guys can somehow reach these drone-building scientists, they might be our best bet. I will admit, I have the NSA keeping close tabs on all such groups in D.C., so I also happen to know that the SWS counts an ex-Chinese national among their ranks. Teaches up at Georgetown, in fact. He was a top researcher for the Chinese government not that long ago, so he might know something about Jinping's plan. It's the best solution I can think of, but we'll need a boat and some volunteers if we're ever going to reach them."

President Obama took another long drag off his cigarette. "I know where there's a boat," he said. "Follow me to Malia's room."

PART 2

The assembled politicians just stared at the President the same way they'd stared at him when he'd first proposed ObamaCare, which is to say like he was out of his fucking mind, but the man knew what he was doing.

With Malia's inflatable Hello Kitty boat in one hand and two life-size cardboard cutouts of the cutest boys from One Direction in the other, Obama held them high above his head like a modern day Moses holding up The Ten Commandments.

"The water is rising, folks," he said to the group, "so here's the plan: Birdman and non-smokers, I need some volunteers to help blow up this boat."

By now the waters had nearly risen to the second story window. They'd be safe for the time being, but if the rain kept falling like it had, there was just no telling how long it would be before the entire White House was underwater.

While Birdman and Senator McCaskill took turns inflating the toy boat as directed, Obama explained his plan to the remaining members of the CTF. Most of them felt that it was a far better idea than Rand Paul's plan to sell off the entire Federal Government, but still pretty crazy.

Crazy all right, but just crazy enough to work.

It was agreed that two senators from each party would take the blow-up boat and try to reach the scientists at Ben's Chili Bowl, which was located in one of the less flooded parts of town. The only question was, would cardboard cutouts of the two cutest boys from One Direction serve as reliable paddles? Some feared that these would disintegrate in the water, if not immediately then certainly over time, but Obama reassured them that the manufacturers of teen idol cutouts had begun triple-laminating their products following complaints to Consumer Reports regarding how poorly they withstood the saliva of tween girls and gay men.

"The girls could take these in the shower with them if they wanted," he said, "but of course we don't allow that sort of thing in the First Family."

For their mission, the Democrats nominated Senator McCaskill, who, after Pelosi's failure, hoped to be the woman that would help save the White House. Chuck Schumer wound up being the other Democrat selected, mainly because the group found him annoying, and he'd begun to feel claustrophobic anyway.

"Anything to get out of this goddamned White House," he said, acting brave.

John McCain volunteered for the Republicans, because he wasn't afraid of death. Marco Rubio decided to throw in as well, knowing that if he helped save the White House, 'Waterbottlegate' would finally be forgotten, leaving him only Governor Christie to beat out for the 2016 presidential nomination.

Meanwhile, the Hello Kitty boat had been fully inflated and was all ready to go, but even the fearless Senator McCain had begun to doubt the wisdom of just cruising right out there with so many sharks still around.

"We head out now," he said, pointing out the window, "we're as good as dead."

"Yeah, I don't feel comfortable leaving just yet," Senator Schumer agreed. "Those sharks are pretty damn close...."

Senator McCaskill nodded. "Chuck is right. We need some kind of diversion. Something to distract them and give us a head start."

"Good idea," said President Obama. "Any volunteers?"

The tension in the group reminded him a bit of Lord of the Flies. Obama may not have been the lord of this group, that much he knew, but he was able to recognize the obvious Piggy in their midst—Bernanke. No one on the CTF really liked the man, and several of its members had already begun to think that he was the most expendable among them.

"What is it?" Bernanke asked, noticing them all staring. "Don't look at me for answers. I still can't think of any way to pay off the Chinese tonight, unless of course you'd like to see an America with the economic stability of Nigeria. I'm already monetizing as much debt as I can!"

"We know," said Harry Reid. "That's why you should be the one to sacrifice yourself, so the Senators can reach those scientists."

Bernanke's breath quickened along with his pulse. "What? No!" he cried. "This is madness, and what about Tim? Geithner is partly to blame for this mess as well! He helped to orchestrate the bailouts, for crying out loud!"

Obama felt a sickness in his stomach. "When you're president," he began, "you have to make tough choices. Personally, I couldn't sleep for days after calling in the attack on Bin Laden, but I still knew that it was the right decision to make. In order for this plan to work, the sharks must be distracted."

"You have got to be fucking kidding me, Barack," Geithner said. "What are we, the fucking Incas now?"

"Tim, you're good man," President Obama said. "I consider you a friend, but it's like that scene in The Godfather II where the man must sacrifice himself. It is true; we are not the Chinese or the Incas. Therefore, you and Ben will not have to kill yourselves."

"Well," Bernanke said, "what sort of sacrifice are we talking about, then?"

"It's simple," Obama continued, "you just need to cut yourselves. The blood in the water should be enough to distract the sharks. You two can do it. All you need to do is lure them over to the other side of the building. That should give the senators all the head start they need to make their escape undetected."

Senator Cruz was none too pleased and shook his head. "Half measures, Obama. I can put a bullet in both of 'em right here and now. Throw 'em to the sharks like chum. My pal Governor Perry, down in Texas, he even accused them of being traitors to our country, so it wouldn't even be illegal."

"No, Cruz," Obama said. "We know how much you Texans like to kill things, but their blood will be enough. Bernanke and Geithner, as your Commander in Chief, I am ordering you to cut yourselves and bleed into the water to distract the sharks. Birdman, you will help them as needed while the senators take the boat into the water."

Bernanke nodded his consent. "Fine," he said, "I can manage this, just keep that crazy cowboy away from me."

Cruz scowled. "I'm no cowboy," he said, "I'm from Canada, dumbass. But I am an American Patriot and you, sir, are a traitor. You and Tim here are the reason why we're in this fucking mess. But fine, at least you'll be shedding blood for your country."

"I dunno," Geithner said. "The mere sight of blood makes me kinda woozy.... And besides, I'm not even supposed to be here tonight. I came out of retirement for this, remember?"

Birdman rolled his eyes. "I'll hold you up, make sure you don't collapse. The three of us, we'll head over to the south side the building. I'll holler when the blood is in the water so the senators can make a fast escape."

"Okay," said President Obama, "Operation Senator Chili Bowl is a go!"

64

Chapter 8

Birdman knelt down, drawing his tactical knife from its ankle sheath as the squeamish former Secretary of the Treasury prepared to get cut. Geithner gulped, nauseated, stomach acid rising up into his esophagus. It was pretty close to the same way he'd felt while solidifying the banks back in '08, but this was a new year and the sharks were far scarier than any CEO of Chase or Wells Fargo he'd ever encountered.

He closed his eyes tight as the agent gripped him by the hand.

"Hold still, Geithner..."

"...Ahh!"

Bernanke watched as Geithner's blood flowed from his sliced thumb and down into the water, dripping thick red drops that were sure to catch the sharks' attention. When his turn came, Birdman had Bernanke roll up his sleeve, trying his forearm instead. As the agent predicted, this produced a much stronger flow of blood, but after about five minutes of bleeding them both, the sharks had still yet to arrive.

It could have been the case that the great whites were more intelligent than the CTF knew, and perhaps they'd caught on to their little blood tricks already, but Birdman had no way of knowing that. All he knew was that if the sharks didn't get over there soon, he'd have to resort to plan B. Their mission was what mattered, and with live bait in the water, Birdman calculated that the senators' chances of escaping the vicinity undetected would increase by nearly 13.3%.

"How come they're not coming?" Bernanke asked, scrutinizing the increasingly bloody water below. He had begun to feel a bit light-headed.

"I dunno..." replied Geithner, himself starting to look a little pale.

"I must've lost... like, a pint of blood already..." Bernanke said.

"Yeah, me too..."

"Bullshit, Tim," Bernanke spat in response, glaring at the rat-faced man beside him. "Don't act like you've bled as much as I have, not with that... tiny fucking thumb wound...."

"Fuck you, Ben," Geithner replied. "You're just trying to throw me... under the bus again, like you did during... the financial crisis...."

"I never threw anyone under the bus..." Bernanke replied with menace in his voice, "but I'm about to throw your skinny ass right out this goddamned window!"

Without further warning, Bernanke attacked Geithner and the two of them began to grapple, doing their awkward best to overpower each other with their weakened, blood-slick arms. It wasn't going so well for either one of them, however, and so Birdman decided to intervene on their behalf.

With one swift kick from his size 17 Oxfords, he sent both of them tumbling over the edge.

Splash!

Stepping up to the windowsill, Birdman looked down upon the flailing economists desperately struggling to drown each other while keeping themselves afloat.

"But why, Agent Birdman?" Bernanke gasped, holding Geithner's head underwater.

Declining to answer, Birdman produced a small metallic canister from inside his coat.

Bernanke screamed as Geithner twisted his nuts underwater, and his victim's head resurfaced.

"Ar-are those... sh-shark pheromones?"

"Very perceptive, former Secretary of the Treasury Geithner."

"Bu-but," stammered Bernanke, his teeth now chattering from the icy water, "ho-how did yo-you get your hands on th-that?"

"You guys clearly don't know much about how the Secret Service operates," Birdman replied with undisguised disdain. "Did you really think my men would miss these PETA plants? Let them lead the sharks right to our President?"

No longer fighting each other, the economists could only huddle together for floatation and warmth, staring up at their executioner with wide, pleading eyes.

"I'm sorry fellas," Birdman continued, casually unscrewing the cap on the canister, "but my job is to protect the President, not a couple of crooked-ass, economy-wrecking, tax-dodging, honky-ass weasels like you."

"Wait, no...!" Bernanke and Geithner both cried out in unison.

"Uh-uh, I don't think so," came Birdman's cold reply. "Ain't nobody gettin' bailed out tonight...."

With that, he casually tossed the canister after them. Suddenly releasing each other, the two men struggled to get as far away from it as possible, but there was just no escaping the potent mix of chemicals as it dissolved into the water.

"Operation Senator Chili Bowl is a go!" Birdman hollered over his shoulder.

Before the sound of his voice had even traveled to the other side of the building, Bernanke's and Geithner's flesh had already been grazed by several different sharks. But it wasn't just blood they were after tonight; aroused by the scent of pheromones, the great whites unfurled their long, retractable dicks and proceeded to gangbang those failed economists like a couple of boiler room bitches.

One of the sharks bit Bernanke's pants right off while another wasted no time getting all up in his pudgy ass. Meanwhile, Geithner had taken a shark cock down his throat with another one wrapped tight around his neck, choking him both from without and within. The horny great whites skewered the men like shish kebabs, fucking them just like they'd previously fucked the United States economy.

Bernanke was actually kind of liking it, at least until the sharks blew their massive loads inside him, simultaneously rupturing his stomach and his bowels with the sudden influx of gallons of great white jizz. Geithner was already dead by the time the sharks were done with him, but his boner was plainly evident for all to see.

Reaching sexual satisfaction, the sharks predictably got hungry again, tearing the men apart like fraudulent pork belly reports on the stock exchange floor.

Meanwhile, Obama had already given the senators his go-ahead. "Okay," he said, "good luck and Godspeed!"

Without a second to lose, they tossed the Hello Kitty boat into the water and boarded it using Malia's play fireman ladder. Birdman ran back over to join his men, providing the senators with additional cover, but for now the sharks were still busy fighting over the scraps of Bernanke's butt cheeks.

Lowering the One Direction cutouts into the boat after them, Obama said a prayer for the senators in hopes that they would reach the scientists safely.

McCain was a Navy man and Rubio had rafting ingrained in his Cuban blood, so the duo paddled furiously, using the young crooners' fabulous hairstyles to power them northward to Ben's Chili Bowl. As if the Chinese could see the progress they were making, the rain began falling even harder on them. Shivering in the middle of the boat, Senators McCaskill and Schumer kept an eye out for shark fins.

McCain's elderly joints and muscles ached from the exertion of paddling, but his old war senses had begun to kick in, giving him the strength and determination to soldier on. His wits hadn't felt this sharp in years.

When his paddle hit something that felt like a rock below, he was ready for the great white that emerged from beneath them.

McCain did not panic at this sneak attack. To him, the shark might as well have been Charlie, and he'd survived the Viet Cong before. Cocking back his fist, the bold AARP member socked the great white square in its black, beady eye. Blood sprayed from the shark's destroyed ocular cavity as it sank back down into the depths.

"Take that, ya Communist bastard!" McCain yelled after it, shaking his fist like he was in a debate.

Meanwhile, the other senators had begun to weep, and for good reason—the wounded shark's blood was sure to attract the others. Before McCain could even lower his angry fist, another great white leapt out of the water, leaving him with nothing but a bloody stump as it sailed on past.

Senator McCaskill shrieked as another shark leapt over their boat, falling into Senator Schumer and knocking him overboard. Valiantly he punched and kicked against the giant great whites as they swarmed all around him, but he was just no match for their sheer size and strength. They ripped him to shreds like Israeli commandos decimating the Gaza Freedom Flotilla.

McCaskill's blood-curdling scream was abruptly cut short

as another great white launched itself completely through her, devouring her entire torso in one savage bite. Her bloody head, arms and legs fell back into the raft with a series of sickening splats.

From the White House, the Secret Service men did their best to counter the sharks with expertly placed sniper rifle shots, but there were just too many of them. Recognizing the futility of their situation and the need to conserve ammo, Obama grimly ordered a cease-fire.

Still, the senators weren't giving up just yet. While Rubio chucked McCaskill's severed limbs out as far as he could, hoping to use them as bait, McCain grabbed up the remnants of her tasteful suit dress, wrapping the tattered fabric around his arm stump like a tourniquet.

For a moment, Rubio wondered just how crazy his Cuban cousins must have been to brave these terrors of the ocean themselves, but quickly he returned his attention to the wounded McCain.

"They've ceased firing, John," he said. "We're screwed, man! Shit, your arm.... You're gonna—"

"What, die?" McCain laughed grimly. "I guess we'll see.... For now, I'm still alive. I've been through worse myself, and your family came over here on rafts, for shit's sake!"

"Yes, sir!" replied Rubio with a salute.

"You are no longer a senator," McCain continued. "You are a soldier of freedom on a mission to reach those scientists. We can do this, Marco." With that, McCain extended his one good hand. "We are Americans, son; we can do anything we put our minds to!"

Rubio went to accept the senator's hand, but he never got to shake it. A shark got ahold of McCain first, dragging him backwards and out of the boat. He disappeared beneath the water's surface like a POW in the jungles of 'Nam, only this time never to resurface again.

Even worse, their inflatable boat had been punctured by a passing shark fin.

As the U.S.S. Hello Kitty slowly sank, a swirling whirlpool of blood and body parts formed around it. No matter what his genetic propensity for water travel, Rubio was officially done for. The sharks chowed him down like a delicious Cuban sandwich at a Miami bodega.

Chapter 9

As the waters began flooding in through the second story window, President Obama was forced to lead the CTF up to the third floor of the White House, his resolve decreasing as the water increased in depth.

Normally in times of trouble, Biden would say something stupid to cheer him up, but with him now gone (along with several other key allies), Obama had begun to feel outnumbered and alone. Besides Boehner, about all he had left were his least favorite Republicans in Congress.

And the worst part about it? He was still supposed to be their leader, and he hadn't the foggiest idea on how to save them, himself, or even their country from these sharks.

With a heavy sigh, Obama sat down on a bed in the servants' quarters and turned on the TV. Perhaps Chris Matthews would elicit some hope, like he had back in 2008, after the Iowa primary victory.

"No thrill running up my leg tonight, folks," Matthews was

saying on MSNBC. "It only just shakes in fear for our beloved President. The stuff I'm hearing about these sharks is just plain... awful. What I want to know is, is the Tea Party involved? They hate the President so much, they just might be willing to work with PETA on this one. Helicopters have attempted a rescue mission, but lightning struck them down as if Zeus himself were a Tea Partier!"

Here, the screen switched to show a satellite image of the White House and its immediate environs. Only its roof remained visible, the East and West Wings completely underwater.

"As you can see, the flooding has inexplicably concentrated itself around the state residence, with waters rising much higher than those being reported in neighboring areas. We still don't know what exactly is causing this climate-change anomaly, but I can only hope that someone, some brave American hero, can reach our President in time."

"Change this clown, would you?" Boehner said.

With very little fight left in him, Obama switched the channel to Fox News.

"I think we clearly need to invade Iran," Brit Hume was saying. "This is clearly the work of radical Muslims who have unleashed fundamentalist Shi'ite sharks upon our nation."

Megyn Kelly flipped her blonde locks and added, "I guess Muslim radicals are now vegans, which makes sense to me. It's probably already in the Quran, and they now have sharks in full jihad mode against the White House tonight. Unfortunately, Obama and the heroes of the Tea Party are going to perish as a result of the President's soft stance on terrorism, palling around with terrorists like PETA and, of course, Bill Ayers."

"And Megyn," Hume interjected, "his cutting of the military budget has certainly come back to haunt him now, hasn't it? The White House is stranded with no defense. The water is rising and so are the number of Al-Qaeda sharks."

"You can change it..." Boehner sighed, crying quietly to

himself as he lit another cigarette. "Too bad Red Eye isn't on. That Greg Gutfeld cheers me up; he's a funny kid. Oh well...."

President Obama decided to shut off the TV altogether. Watching cable news was like tonguing a canker sore on the roof of his mouth, a distraction that offered no solutions and only made their problems somehow feel even worse.

Still, without the background noise of those talking heads yammering on, Obama could actually hear the water rising all around them, and his fear only rose with it. After successfully assassinating Bin Laden earlier that year, he'd seen himself as protector of the people, one with great strength. Now though, he just felt like a wimp, a girly man from Hawaii where young boys grew up with acute shark phobia.

Some Polynesians believed the great whites to be fallen angels, cast down from Heaven along with Lucifer, only to become arch demons of the sea. Obama did not fear much, but being eaten alive by one of those monsters was something that had pervaded his every waking thought, even before this catastrophe. He wondered if the Chinese had done a psychological profile on him to figure this out, using his weaknesses against him.

Such thoughts were pointless, he realized. There was no more room for conjecture or half-assed solutions. Rather, he'd have to get at the source of the problem, at least if he expected to save his nation and its government tonight.

Obama took a look around the room, considering all the tired, broken faces he saw.

"Birdman," he said, turning to the door.

"Yeah?" the agent replied, poking his head in from the hall.

"I'll require your assistance in setting up another comm channel. Time is of the essence."

Birdman seemed genuinely surprised. "You're actually going to try talking with that nutjob again?"

Senator Sanders suddenly began to retch, dry heaving in

the corner.

"Yes," Obama confirmed, "I'm going to talk to the President of China about paying off our debt."

"But why?" asked Michelle Bachmann, momentarily breaking her prayer trance. "He's clearly insane!" She then went back to speaking in tongues.

"Because if I don't, we'll die."

"Well, I'm all for it," said Senator Paul, his mood noticeably brightened. "Maybe you can save us and the taxpayers tonight!"

Like Sanders, Obama also felt sick to his stomach, but this didn't stop him from switching on the satellite feed after the comm link had been established. This issue was more important than the Affordable Health Care Act, the impending fiscal cliff, and his birth certificate all rolled up into one. And if he failed to resolve it tonight, he would likely go down in history as the worst president ever, not to mention the first one eaten by sharks.

And it was becoming increasingly evident that he was all on his own.

Before they got a visual, the CTF could hear the sound of classical music coming in through the TV's speakers. When President Jinping finally appeared onscreen, he was seated upon his golden throne once again, this time playing a Beethoven concerto on violin.

"President Jinping," Obama addressed him, "if I could please have your attention, sir."

Finishing the final measure with a flourish, the Chinese leader lowered his bow and smiled brightly at the camera. "Oh, hello again President Obama," he said. "I'm glad to see you still alive. I trust you have good news for me?"

"Yes," Obama replied. "I'm going to work with the Republican Congress to pay off our debt to your nation; we should have a deal figured out before the end of the night. But first, could you call off this rain?"

"So, Mr. Obama..." the Chinese leader replied, setting his

violin off to the side, "the Hawaiian in you feels the pressure, no? Though we Chinese respect hard sciences more, psychology is quite good too, as we do love our Jung.... With name like that, I believe he may have been Chinese Jew? Good with brain and money, not like you Americans. Hahaha!"

They DID do a profile on me, Obama thought to himself, ignoring the Jinping's remarks. "Look," he said, "we have come to the table, but you need to stop with the rain, the sharks, and the lightning here tonight. I want us to discuss how to pay off this debt, but with all of these dangers constantly surrounding us, I'm afraid we'll all be dead before we're able to come up with a solution. It's been very distracting."

The Chinese President called for his cat and she jumped into his lap. "Ah, yes..." he said, gently stroking her head. "Just like cat want pet right now, China want pay right now. You pay now, President Obama!"

"Ummm... President Jinping?"

This time it was Senator Harry Reid who spoke up.

"Huh? Yes?"

"You realize how... uhh... racist you sound, right?"

"What sound racist?"

"Well, the way you keep saying 'you pay now!', for instance. It's like you're speaking stereotypical, broken Chinglish for some reason, and, well, you're supposed to be the leader of your country. Whether you like it or not, you represent the people of China. All of them."

"How it racist if way I talk?!" came Jinping's sharp retort. "Not all Chinese talk pretty white tongue like snobby American Senator, you know. Can I help if way I sound?!"

"Wait, that's not—"

"Who racist now, Senator Reid, hmmmm? You want I should call PC Police on White House, too? That what you want?!"

"President Jinping, please understand," said President Obama, trying to get things back on track. "Under these conditions, it will be very hard for us to come up with any kind of reasonable economic plan. We need you to meet us halfway here, before we'll be able to give you what you want."

"No," was Jinping's cold reply. "We do not stop rain and we not stop sharks, Mr. Obama. You must feel the pressure...." The Chinese President looked from Obama to Senator Paul and smiled. "I see you back there, Mr. Paul. You look quite pleased with plan; you'd make good American President. You would pay down debt and not stick nose where it no belong!"

"Please, President Jinping," Obama said. "I implore you to listen to reason."

But the Chinese leader was not listening anymore. "Ahhh..." he sighed. "I can hear the raindrops falling on your side; can you not? You better hurry, President Obama, or you and top leaders will be toppings on Hawaiian shark pizza tonight...."

"Wait, President Jinping!

"Bai bai...."

The feed cut out and President Obama looked over at Rand Paul, who couldn't help but shrug his shoulders and smile.

"Though a crazed Communist," the senator began, "Jinping does make some good points. It looks like we're finally going to have to cut these entitlement programs after all, at least if we expect to make it out of this alive. But not that's not all, of course. We'll need to cut most of our big government bureaucracies as well. In fact, to start, I'd like to suggest cutting the Department of Homeland Security, as they obviously have not been doing a very good job."

President Obama bummed another cigarette from Speaker Boehner as Paul began listing all the things he'd be nominating for the chopping block.

Chapter 10

President Obama continued chain smoking deep into the night. His need for soothing nicotine spiked with each essential program Paul proposed they cut. They had Eric Cantor gleefully doing the math on some scraps of paper.

They had already trimmed a whole bunch of smaller items from the federal budget when the two biggies finally came up, Medicare and Social Security.

"I'm sorry, but we can no longer afford to continue funding Medicare and Social Security," Paul explained, "at least not the way they are now. But if we raise the age of eligibility to 92, we can probably keep it mostly intact and still pay off our debts."

Senator Bernie Sanders shook like a bomb about to explode, his face turning red with anger. "Let me get this straight," he growled between clenched teeth. "We're going to cut the entire annual budget of the Department of Labor, the Department of Education, the FDA, the EPA, and one quarter of the Department of Defense, and on top of that you dare to go after

Medicare and Social Security as well? This is an outrage! I won't let it happen."

Rand Paul appeared unfazed, combing his fingers through his dubious curls.

"Instead of the chickens coming home to roost," he said, "it's sharks this time. Our federal spending has literally caused blood in the water here tonight. Everything has to be on the table, Bernie. As a Socialist I know you'd probably prefer to keep adding things to our debt, but the reality is that we need to reverse this wasteful trend in government spending."

"Listen, you Ayn Rand-reading buffoon," Senator Sanders countered, "you want to cut Medicare and Social Security, you'll have to do it over my dead body!"

"Well, sir, with all due respect," Senator Paul snapped back, "that option is also on the table if the sharks have anything to say about it."

Senator Sanders just shook his head in disbelief. "Barack, you would really let this happen?" he asked. "Even Social Security— the program that helped out your nice but racist grandmother?"

"Um, look, Bernie," Obama began, searching for the words. "Maybe Rand has a point. Maybe some of this government spending really has been irresponsible after all. We need to consider all options if we're going to come up with the money we owe, so unless we're willing to compromise here, we're all going to be shark food sooner or later."

"But what about the folks who depend on Social Security and Medicare to survive?" Senator Sanders sputtered. "They'll all be dead by the time they're eligible under this fool's draconian plan!"

"Enough with the debate," Rand Paul said, "the free market will take care of these problems. That's why we cut spending and taxes as well; it's a win-win for everyone."

Senator Sanders took his favorite locally bought, fair-trade shoe and kicked a chair over in frustration. He was not a violent person at heart, but Paul's increasingly ludicrous suggestions had begun to bring out his inner Occupier.

"Obama, this can't seriously be happening!" he objected. "He's going to cut taxes, sure, but probably mostly for the rich, and you know they pay much less than their fair share already. This is like Reaganomics part two!"

A flash of lightning illuminated the room, casting long, ominous shadows of shark fins in silhouette against the wall. The flood waters showed no signs of receding, poised to swallow the White House whole, and the great whites were closing in on their position. Pretty soon they'd have nowhere left to run.

"I'm afraid there's not much else we can do at this point, Bernie," Obama said. "The Paul Agenda is the only feasible solution right now. Maybe his tax cuts can at least keep our economy from turning out like Greece."

"President Obama," Sanders said, "I may have chosen you over Hillary before, but underneath all your slickness, I now see a man who is just like her husband: an opportunistic smooth talker, unwilling to die for his beliefs. Well, I said it once and I'll say it again: I'd rather be thrown to the sharks than cut Medicaid and Social Security! At least one of us is willing to die for what we believe in...."

Turning away from the President in utter disgust, he began his solemn march to the window. There were sharks right outside, he could see them in the rising water, and they were going to help him make good on his promise.

"No, Bernie!" Obama screamed. "Don't commit shark-suicide! When the sharks are all gone, we can figure out a way to start a new Social Security, together!"

"There will always be sharks, Mr. President," Sanders replied, his voice trembling with idealistic anger as he raised the window open. "It is your job not to feed them with the corpses of the poor."

"Wait, no!"

Senator Bernie Sanders jumped out the window, making a soft splash as the water had risen to the third floor of the White House. He felt in his heart that he made the right choice but his survival instincts took over. Sanders waded through the debris and found a floating billboard of his least favorite capitalist fast food place—McDonald's.

He maneuvered on top, near the board's French fries, like Rose in Titanic, and looked down at them feeling grateful. He wondered if private enterprise ever served any good, but before he could contemplate an answer, a hungry great white shark broke through the billboard and Senator Bernie Sanders became an unhappy meal.

PART 3

Chapter 11

The few surviving politicians huddled close together in the servant's quarters, feverishly debating while the rain hammered down and negotiations continued over what to cut from the federal budget.

From across the huddle, President Obama regarded Senator Paul with a grumpy cat-like frown. Meanwhile, Paul couldn't help but crack a smile now and then, excited by the prospect of his lifelong dream—drastically reducing the size of the Federal Government—finally coming true. He'd never felt much affection for sharks before, but they'd since become his official favorite animal amongst all God's creatures.

Obama felt powerless in this discussion, measuring his own gloom against Paul's barely concealed glee. The only other liberal left among them was Senator Reid, who'd apparently turned on his principles as well.

"I don't like it either, Mr. President," he said, "but we need to survive this. We will find our way toward a more prosperous future for America. Until that day arrives, I am ready to support the Paul Plan."

Obama finished his cigarette and bummed another one from Boehner. "Before we officially go through with the Paul Plan," he said, "I'd like to FaceTime with my family and talk to Michelle and the girls. For those of you with a working phone and people you care about, I suggest you do the same. For better or worse, we are about to fundamentally transform America as we know it."

"Good idea," Michele Bachmann said. "I need to talk to my husband and tell him that I love him, and also make sure he's not going to those bathhouses he loves so much. I tell ya, he wastes a fortune on those damn saunas."

The other CTF members took out their phones as well, but only President Obama's had enough bars for a connection. On the second ring, Michelle's relieved face appeared on his screen.

"Barack!" she cried. "Oh, baby.... Thank goodness you're alive! The girls and I were worried sick when we couldn't get through to you! What's going on down there?"

"Well, first of all," Obama replied, "thank God you took them to see that new Disney movie tonight. It's bad here, my love."

"Are there really sharks? That's what my NPR app said. Right now the girls and I are stranded at the theater in northwest D.C. The storm was bad, and there's been flooding all over town, but nothing like what's being reported down there. They're saying that the tsunami washed in a flood of sharks, and that the White House is almost entirely underwater!"

"It's true, Michelle. PETA and China are behi..." he trailed off. "Well, you wouldn't believe it anyway. I swear, it's like something out of one of those movies your cousin would watch on SyFy while drinking Olde English on Saturdays."

"Oh my god, Barack! This is terrible! I heard they got Joe.... Are you sure you're okay?"

"It's true. They did. But I'm managing, dear."

"I know how much you fear those sharks, baby," she sighed. "I'm so sorry.... I wish I could come and rescue you myself, but we can see the lightning from here, and it looks just... unreal. The flooding, too... like somehow it's all been concentrated around the White House. This weather... do you think it might be being controlled by someone? One of our enemies? That's another rumor that's been going around. Some say it's Al-Qaeda."

"That's classified information, my dear," Obama replied. "Trust me—you don't even want to know. All I can say is that the water continues to rise, and the only way we can stop it is by making some tough choices to pay off our debt to China tonight. At this point..." he paused, about to say the unthinkable, "I think we're going to have to get rid of the Federal Government."

"Get rid of it?"

"Yes, get rid of it."

"That doesn't make any sense, Barack. Constitutionally, I don't even know if that's even possible."

"It is. There are loopholes we're exploiting, and pretty much all governmental departments will have to be gutted or disbanded. If we don't, well... there's just no telling what these sharks will do to this country once they're through with us."

"You're the President, Barack, and I love you, but you just can't do this. You can't!"

"I'm afraid I must. We'll all be eaten by sharks, probably you and the girls too, if we don't do something to stop them tonight."

"Baby, I know that our government is a mess, but it does do some good for the people. You can't just disband the Federal Government because of a terrorist shark attack."

"I'm sorry, honey. Please forgive me, but these are bioengineered great whites we're talking about here. 'White demons', like my old Polynesian friend Mai'o used to call them. They're going to start with us, and then they'll probably eat the rest of America if we don't act now."

"Barack, you chose to be president, but you're not acting like one right now. You're acting like a little punk-ass bitch, just like when you refused to go swimming in the ocean last time we were in Hawaii. Baby, you need to do what's right; not what's safe. You are not just this family's protector, you are this country's protector as well."

"But honey...."

"But honey nothing. Stop being a bitch, Barack. Your father didn't herd goats so you could sell out the American dream to these sharks."

"My father was a brave man... he would tell me to tough it out. He even faced lions as a shepherd."

"I know he would; even your white momma would say the same."

"I know.... You're right, Michelle. Damn it, honey, you're always right. I will not let these terrorists intimidate me into destroying our nation!"

"You're damn straight, baby. And don't you even think about trying to cut my 'Let's Move' campaign! I'll make those sharks look like Little Nemo if you do."

"I won't, honey. I will do what's right for this country."

"Now that's the Barack I married and knew would make a fine president one day."

"Thank you, dear. Say a prayer for me, and if I don't make it out of this alive, just know that I love you three with all my heart."

"I love you, too, honey. Just do what's right, Barack. Ride the wave of justice, even if it means the end."

"Thanks, Michelle. If I could, I would give you a fist bump right now."

"You will, after this. Just survive and have faith. Have faith that you can still do what's right for your country."

"I love you, Michelle. I will."

"I love you, too, Barack."

With that, President Obama closed his FaceTime app, feeling a renewed sense of purpose. He was not going to sacrifice his ideals, and if he had to sacrifice anything, he would follow Senator Sander's brave example before he'd eviscerate his own government. He was the President of the United States, and he was ready to start acting like it.

Obama returned to the ongoing huddle more energized and determined than ever before.

"Okay, Senator Paul," he began, "let's discuss the reality of the situation. We do need to enact some major reforms. That much is clear, but we can't just slash our social safety nets and expect that the most disadvantaged members of society won't fall through the cracks. If you think government spending is irresponsible, think about that for a second. Instead, we can do a combo of the Simpson-Bowles Plan and the old Paul Ryan Plan, paying off China over time, but we cannot give in to their demands by paying up everything now."

"Mr. President," Senator Paul replied, his voice darkening in tone. "I think that maybe you have been hit on the head or something, and are incapable of making good decisions for this group. Frankly, I think that I should assume the role of acting President, because with the way you're talking, you're going to get us all killed."

Eric Cantor had also been reveling in the unrestrained spending cuts up until that point, and while he didn't exactly appreciate the President's sudden backpedaling either, he did believe in following constitutional protocol.

"I think that's a great idea, Senator Paul," he said, "but procedure states that it would be Speaker Boehner to make the decision. What do you say, John? Are you ready to finally make the Tea Party proud, save our lives, and become our new President?"

Congressmen Boehner lit up another cigarette. "Fuck no!" he coughed in response. "President Obama is the rightful leader of the United States. I may be a no-nonsense conservative, but I'm not selling the few decent social programs we have left to pay off those Communist bastards. And if that means I get eaten by sharks too, then so be it."

President Obama high-fived Speaker Boehner in a gesture of solidarity, but Rand Paul could only seethe in his own impotent rage. Suddenly jumping up onto the table, he pointed an angry finger down at them. "Obama, you're a fool!" he cried at the top of his lungs. "I'm telling you, this bloated Federal Government will be the death of us al—"

Cutting him off in more ways than one, an enormous great white burst through the floorboards directly underneath him, snapping both the table and the senator in half between its gnashing, bloody jaws.

Chapter 12

While the upper half of Senator Paul continued mumbling on about fiscal responsibility, trailing guts behind him as he crawled along the floor, another shark burst in from below, nearly maiming Eric Cantor in similar fashion. Michelle Bachmann screamed bloody murder and Ted Cruz yelled "HOLY SHIT!!!", and the entire room erupted into chaos.

Birdman and his two remaining agents opened fire on the sharks as the water rushed up through the holes they'd created. Caught in the arm by a tail fin, one of the Secret Service men immediately dropped his gun. He was snagged by a shark diving after it, but Congresswoman Bachmann swiftly grabbed it up instead. Pulling the trigger again and again, she took aim for the sharks' mouths and eyes, which were practically the only weak points in their thick, coarse skin.

Meanwhile, Senator Cruz struggled to reload his revolver, dropping the last of his remaining bullets between shaking fingers. Looking on helplessly as the shark shook the agent like a dog with chew toy, he threw his gun at the monster instead and bolted for the door.

Unfortunately, however, he tripped on Rand Paul's intestines, which were floating around his ankles. Falling face-first into the water, he landed right in the path of the other shark's ravenous maw, and his legs were eaten off along with his favorite studs from bootbarn.com.

By the time another shark broke through the floor, the water had already risen to their knees. Bachmann saw that she didn't stand a chance. While the other two sharks fought over Senator Cruz's torso, she tried to run as well, but this latest arrival blocked her escape. Dropping to her knees as the great white lunged at her, she curled up into a tiny ball and prayed to God that he'd turn her into a female Jonah.

He might have heard her prayer as she was swallowed whole, instantly entombed within the shark's spacious stomach. Surrounding Bachmann were the partially digested limbs and entrails of earlier victims. She tried to scream, but only succeeded in getting a mouthful of stomach acid instead. She felt as though she'd gone to Hell itself as the digestive juices burned into her skin.

Panicking, she began firing blind, hoping to hit one of the shark's vital organs from within. Just before she perished, she managed to score a lucky shot on its heart, finally doing some good for the White House as the twenty-four-foot great white flopped dead on its side.

President Obama stood behind Birdman, who was running low on bullets by this point. They watched from across the room as a shark swam after Harry Reid, who tried holding up his Book of Mormon as a form of defense. Neither one of them were very surprised when the great white ate the LDS senator right along with his holy book.

Moments later, the final Secret Service agent got taken out as well, crushed between jaws that knew neither satiation nor mercy. Undaunted, Birdman continued firing at the sharks, but House Majority Leader Eric Cantor already knew that bullets would not be enough to stop them. Luckily though, he had an idea of something that would.

No one in Washington had a clue, not even his closest aides, but Cantor was addicted to shooting up cocaine and was an avid user of steroids as well. He'd kept this secret all throughout his political career, hiding his track marks and muscles beneath loose-fitting suits, but tonight it was time to finally come clean.

Grabbing a syringe from his briefcase and spiking it full of liquid cocaine, he then selected another one that had already been fully juiced with 'roids. Wielding them like daggers in each fist, he stunned the nearest shark with an anabolically enhanced punch to the snout and hopped up onto its back. Jabbing both needles into its black, beady eyes, the potent mixture of drugs gave the great white a massive seizure on the spot, leaving it twitching and near death beneath him.

He already had several more syringes loaded up and ready to go, but instead of distributing these to Obama and Boehner, Cantor decided to keep them for himself. Convinced that he'd make a much better president than the two of them combined, he'd already determined that he would be the one to carry out the Paul Plan, paying off their Chinese debt if he survived.

There was still one shark left to deal with, though. Getting desperate as his last clip neared empty, Birdman's eyes cast about the debris in the rising water, searching for anything he could use as a weapon. A fire extinguisher had floated within reach, which he quickly snatched up and took a look at its label.

"Made in China!" he yelled over his shoulder to Obama. "These are the dangerous ones!" He grinned at the President and said, "No safety seal on these!"

Obama couldn't believe that his own personal safety equipment could be so unsafe, making a mental note to set up better regulations for that in the future. Still, he'd be happy if it paid off at the moment.

Holding the fire extinguisher in front of him like a battering ram, Birdman waited for his chance to strike. When the last shark predictably lunged for him, he made his move, shoving the pressurized vessel into its mouth. He then grabbed President Obama and Speaker Boehner, dragged them both behind a nearby couch, and hollered, "GET DOWN!!!"

Popping up over the back of the sofa, Birdman took aim and his aim was true. He nailed the defective extinguisher with his very last bullet, exploding the shark's head into a white and red cloud of foam and blood, sending razor sharp teeth and bone fragments flying in all directions.

"AHHHHHHHHHH!!!"

Looking down at his mutilated body, Eric Cantor stared aghast at the gaping wounds inflicted by the shark shrapnel, dropping his fistfuls of syringes as the blood began pouring out of him.

Besides Cantor, it was down to Birdman, Obama, and Boehner by that point. He shot them a pleading look from across the room as he slumped against the wall and another shark emerged from the depths, but they couldn't have helped him then even if they'd wanted to. He had been a man who kept things from getting done in Washington, always holding up legislation with his petty and illogical objections, and finally it all made sense—he hadn't been drunk on power as once believed; he'd been high on cocaine and steroids.

Rearing up like Jaws on a movie poster, the great white tore into his muscle-bound, teeth-riddled body, dragging it back down into the hole where it came from, probably to OD on his drug-laced blood.

The three survivors swiftly exited the servant's quarters, knowing full well that they could not remain on this floor any longer. Birdman led the way to the only place left for them—the White House roof.

Chapter 13

Up on the roof, they may have been safe from the sharks for now, but they still had the elements to weather. Reaching into his coat, Birdman produced a telescoping umbrella, opening it up in a vain attempt to at least keep them dry while they waited out the last bit of their lives. With any luck, he thought, they might get struck by lightning before the sharks' next attack.

When they felt the first few bumps beneath their feet, they knew it was only a matter of time before the sharks would be on them once again, leaving the survivors with nowhere left to go but down into their flesh-gorged bellies at last.

Taking out his phone with trembling hands, Obama found that he still had a few bars of reception and a little bit of battery left. "Might as well check the news," he said, trying to overcome his sense of resignation. "Maybe something's been reported. Maybe they're still coming for us. Who knows? Maybe a miracle will happen after all."

"Still got nothing, sir," Birdman responded, sadly shaking

his head. He took out his earpiece and tossed it out into the water. "You won't hear anything good, I assure you."

"Don't be so pessimistic," Obama said, holding up his phone. "I ran a successful campaign on hope, you might remember, and I'm not about lose it all just yet."

The President launched his MSNBC app and waited for Chris Matthews' face to appear onscreen. "It seems the President and Congress are doomed, folks," Matthews remarked. "There will be no more Federal Government after this, and the Tea Party is going to commemorate the occasion with a national holiday, just you wait. At this point, with the White House surrounded by sharks and almost entirely underwater, it seems unlikely that our armed forces will be able to save them in time."

Obama switched from MSNBC to Fox, where they were comparing the credentials and accomplishments of various Republican congressmen. "There may be hope for our President yet," Brit Hume was presently saying, "but since he's probably dead already, along with all of the other high-ranking members of Congress, the question we should really be asking is who will take his place?"

"Look, Brit, I don't mean to be insensitive here," Bill O'Reilly chimed in, "but this could be a blessing in disguise, this terrorist shark attack. Though my thoughts go out to the Obamas here tonight, our government needs a new change. I mean, how can we trust a White House that can't even protect itself?"

Obama felt like throwing his phone off the roof right then and there, but even in times of crisis he was capable of controlling such emotions. Shutting it off instead, he looked over at Boehner and said, "You know what? Both our sides are full of shit."

Boehner lit his last two cigarettes and handed one to Obama. "They certainly are," he was willing to agree, "but you wanna know something else, Barack? We're not. You and me, we get shit on by everyone out there, but we're just men who've tried to do what we feel is best for America. Though it may be too late for us, at least we didn't wind up selling our country off to China. Then we'd be even worse than those assholes on TV."

Obama laughed, blowing smoke. "This might be the first time I regret not having the press around."

Boehner laughed, too. "Sure!" he said. "There are a few of them I wouldn't mind tossing overboard myself."

Obama took another drag as the rain continued to fall.

"But in all seriousness, you know the CTF was doomed from the start in this kind of toxic political environment. Kinda puts this whole thing in perspective, but I guess it just is what it is."

"Yup," Boehner agreed. "It is what it is...."

"Tell you what," Obama said, "I'm gonna try getting President Jinping on FaceTime right now, so we can tell him not to expect our payment tonight after all; that we'll pay our debt eventually, just not right now, no matter what he wants to throw at us. God willing, if we survive this, you and I can finally propose a budget that makes sense for this great nation, and then we'll never have to borrow another dime from those evildoers ever again."

Boehner laughed and said, "You sound a lot like Bush right now, with that kind of talk."

"John, I'm tolerant man, and I don't fear much in life except for pissing off Michelle and great white sharks. But I will tell you this: Jinping is an evil man, and we will have to work with all our might to compete against his country in the future. Damn Huntsman, he tried to warn me! It's why he ran against me, you know."

"He tried to warn us all," Boehner replied, "but he came off as too smart and too much of a pussy for my base to vote for him. Next time, we'll listen. For right now, let's get Jinping on the phone. This might be the last chance we'll ever have to tell that crazy son of a bitch where to stick it. They can go on eating their tofu, but if we do somehow manage to get out of this alive, you and I can come up with a debt plan over a couple of good steaks and a pack of Marlboros. What do you say?"

"Sounds like a plan, John." Obama said. "Birdie, we're not giving up just yet, so we need your support as well. I want to eat that steak with John here and kiss my girls and wife."

"Yes sir," Birdman said, doing his best to power through.

President Obama flicked his butt into the water and dialed up the Chinese President on FaceTime. When Jinping appeared onscreen, he was eating yet another bowl of ToFin soup.

"Ah, President Obama, you are still alive," he said, putting down his bowl and wiping his lips. "But you are on roof! It will not be long before sharks reach roof, you know.... That like American song—raise roof, right? Hahaha! Ohhhhhh, I so funny...."

"Listen, Jinping," Obama said, "we've officially had enough of your shit, if you'll pardon my language. Speaker Boehner and I have agreed to jointly pen a bill to pay off our debt, but it will take us at least ten years to do so. Anything else is just unfeasible."

"Ten years?" Jinping replied. "You pay in ten minutes, or I make sharks raise roof."

Boehner was incapable of holding back his tears any longer, but Barack's anger was stronger than his fear.

"You do what you gotta do," he said with confidence. "When history looks back at us, we will be the Spartans, and you will be the Persians."

"I said..." President Jinping replied, taking out his weather remote once again, "this! Is! China! We Sparta; you Persia, fools. No matter... Now you die!"

With that he pressed the button, and the three men braced for another tsunami.

Chapter 14

But the tsunami didn't come. In fact, if anything, the storm finally seemed to be letting up a bit. When the darkness of the sky was next illuminated by a flash of light, it definitely wasn't lightning that time, and the next loud noise they heard rolling over the water definitely wasn't thunder.

It was a searchlight, and a boat horn.

President Jinping clicked his weather remote again and again, cursing at the lack of results. "What is it?" he demanded to know, watching the look of elation spread across Obama's face. "What you looking at?"

"It's... a miracle...."

The Chinese President threw a tantrum on his end of the line, but was soon cut off by an incoming call to Obama from Senator John Kerry.

"John F. Kerry, reporting for duty, sir."

Peering into the light as the boat drew closer, John Boehner shielded his eyes with a tan hand to get a better look at it.

Borrowing Birdman's binoculars, he saw that, sure enough, it was John Kerry himself, sporting a captain's cap aboard his yacht. Joining him were half a dozen nerdy-looking, middle-aged men in black t-shirts with the red letters SWS printed on them.

"Well, I'll be damned..." Boehner said, "it is Kerry! And it looks like he's brought the Scientists With Swag along with him. Do you... do you think that they somehow managed to stop the storm...?" He trailed off with a sniffle here, shedding tears of joy for the first time that evening.

"Tell me something good, Kerry," Obama said into his phone.

"Mr. President," Kerry began, "I'll get straight to the point. I'd heard rumors about the Chinese working on some sort of weather manipulation technology some time ago, from my contacts in the NSA."

"Why didn't anyone tell me this?"

"I don't know. Maybe because they got tired of presidents routinely ignoring their warnings about looming terrorist threats?"

President Obama frowned, but then he remembered his predecessor's foreknowledge of 9/11. "Go on," he said.

"Anyway, once I saw this storm rolling in, I combined the experience I'd gained in the Navy with my own proclivities as an avid yachter, along with my deep knowledge of weather patterns. And the only conclusion I could come to was that this storm seemed... unnatural, to say the least."

Navigating his yacht around the jagged stump of the Washington Monument, Kerry was only just a block away.

"Mr. Kerry," Obama said, "it seems you missed our meeting and inadvertently wound up being the smartest man not in the room by being dumb enough to go out sailing in that storm. What else have you been able to learn?"

"Earlier today," Kerry replied, "I took the Flipper-Flopper here out on the Potomac to investigate further; that's when I discovered the sharks."

"And why didn't you warn us then?" Obama asked.

"I tried to get the word out, but the storm was already picking up and my communications inexplicably went down. It seems all these Chinese electronics have been working against us, conveniently falling when we need them most. Anyway, as I made my way back in your direction, the storm worsened dramatically, and I knew that something wasn't right. That's when I decided that I had to go and find Al Gore."

"Gore. Of course," Obama said. "He's the weather expert. Good choice."

"Yup," Kerry continued, "found him up at Ben's Chili Bowl with the SWS. Initially he assumed the freak tsunami had been caused by global warming, but the Chinese defector in the group was able to confirm that China had in fact been actively experimenting with weather control. He had been the one to draw up the original design of Jinping's remote himself, so he already knew its flaws."

"And you have these men with you now?"

"I do, including former Vice President Gore. They are busy jamming Jinping's weather frequencies as we speak. Soon we will be the ones controlling the weather, not China!"

"Wonderful, Senator Kerry. I'm glad we'll get to greet these heroes momentarily. But do you think you could step on it a bit?" As he said this, the first giant shark fin broke up through the roof. "I'm afraid we're not quite out of this yet."

"Just a moment, Mr. President."

Spotting a great white caught in a massive tangle of plastic bags up ahead, Kerry went full throttle, ramming the Flipper-Flopper right over it. Then, just to make sure the shark was dead, he efficiently backed his engine blades into it, showering the surrounding water with thick cuts of shark sashimi.

"How's that for a swiftboating?" he chuckled to himself.

"Excuse me? Kerry?"

"Yes, sir. Sorry."

"I'm still not sure how this whole thing can be stopped," Obama continued, stepping to the side as another fin burst through the roof nearby. "And while the weather does appear to be clearing, I do remain concerned about these sharks."

"The scientists will stop them," Kerry reassured him. "In fact," he said, checking his watch, "their SWS drones should be on their way back from destroying the Chinese weather nodes and comm jammers off the coast as we speak. I think you'll be seeing them soo—ooh, and here they are!"

Expertly manipulating the joysticks on their American-built radio controllers, the scientists flew their drones over the Flipper-Flopper in 'V' formation, whereupon they immediately began delivering their payloads to the great white sharks surrounding the White House. Great geysers of crimson red water blasted up wherever their precision strikes connected, making short work of the beasts.

President Obama smiled from the roof; he did love him some drones, and as he watched them decimate the sharks with government surplus Hellfire missiles, he loved them even more.

"Thank you, Senator Kerry," he said into his phone. "You make your country proud once again. Now, if you'll excuse me, I have to finish a conversation with an enemy of the United States."

"Yes, sir," Kerry replied before hanging up. He was just then pulling up alongside the White House.

Switching back over to FaceTime, Obama regarded Jinping with something almost like pity, so sad and disappointed did the Chinese President look. He almost felt bad holding his phone out seaward, presenting him with the gory scene of shark carcasses floating everywhere.

Meanwhile, up on deck, Al Gore and was complaining to an Indian scientist controlling one of the drones.

"Don't get me wrong," he said, "it's good we're saving the

President with drones and all, but do you have any idea how bad their emissions are?"

The scientist just gave him a look of mild annoyance, which quickly morphed into one of sheer terror as a thirty-foot great white emerged from the water behind him.

Closing its jaws around his upper half, the shark removed Gore's own carbon footprint from the planet with one savage bite.

All that was left of the former Vice President were his legs, dangling off the starboard side of the Flipper-Flopper like a couple of hanging chads.

Chapter 15

The few remaining sharks fought over Gore's corpse as Birdman, Obama, and Boehner boarded Kerry's yacht. The President mourned for his friend, his mentor, and his all-time favorite filmmaker, but this did little to dampen the overwhelming sense of happiness he felt watching the drones rain death from above. For the first time that night, the waters surrounding the White House shimmered crimson with shark instead of human blood.

"So, President Jinping," Obama said, "what do you think of our drones? I'd say your sharks were no match for the Scientists With Swag."

"Well, I guess not all Americans hamburger-eating morons after all..." Jinping conceded.

"No, President Jinping, they are not. They are chili-eating geniuses, and we'll find more of them, just you wait. I'm afraid, sir, that your plan has been thwarted."

"Has it, Obama?"

Panning out across the sea of dead sharks bobbing and bleeding around their boat, the President provided him with all the evidence he could ever need. Off in the distance, the very last shark could be seen trying to swim away to freedom. The SWS weren't having any of that shit, though. Catching it in the spotlight of a pursuing drone, they sent one final missile right up its bunghole, exploding it into a ball of righteous American fire.

As Obama turned the camera back around on himself, Jinping caught a glimpse of Birdman, who gave the Chinese President the finger.

"Birdie, not appropriate," Obama said. "But this one time I'll let it slide." He then looked back to Jinping and asked, "Did you get a better look that time, Mr. President?"

"My poor, beautiful sharks..." the Chinese leader sighed despondently. "PETA, too—they will be so sad...."

"We're putting PETA on our list of active terrorist groups," Obama said. "Their leaders, along with Al-Qaeda's, are now considered war criminals."

"That fine," Jinping replied. "I really no like ToFin soup anyways. PETA not complete promise of delicious, cruelty-free shark substitute."

"Well, President Jinping," Obama continued, "I have a promise for you: America will not soon forget this unprovoked attack, and considering all the damage you've done here tonight, we won't be paying you a single cent."

"Really, Mr. President," the Chinese leader replied, "I think there one more thing you should know...."

"I'm afraid not," Obama said, cutting him off. "I don't need to know anything more from you. We aren't paying you jack, and we now have scientists with more knowledge of weather control than even you do. We will right our nation's course now that your sharks have been stopped, and America will be great once again."

"But President Obama, I must tell you about super—"

"The only thing that is super, sir, is America," Obama said, cutting him off again. "With all due respect, there is nothing super about China anymore. You and your government are true evildoers, just another washed-up Communist enemy still butthurt over losing the Cold War. We beat Communism before, and we will beat it again. Goodbye, sir."

With that, Obama hung up the phone. He knew it wasn't his finest speech, but it was easily the most sincere and inspired thing he'd ever said that didn't involve a teleprompter. The others onboard applauded his brave demonstration of American exceptionalism, and Obama responded by saying, "God Bless America!"

Blowing its horn triumphantly, the Flipper-Flopper pulled away from the White House and set a course for Freedom.

Chapter 16

The remaining survivors relaxed on aboard the Flipper-Flopper. Obama hugged Kerry and the Scientists With Swag, holding the men close and hard, but releasing them before it became awkward. Boehner also took it upon himself to embrace these unlikely heroes.

"You... you saved us," he wept into one man's shoulder. "You saved our asses and you saved America."

The scientists humbly bowed their heads to the President and the Speaker of the House as Birdman kept watch on deck.

"It's quite all right, Agent Birdman," Kerry said, sipping champagne as he placed an arm around his tense shoulders. "The drones have eliminated every shark in the vicinity. You can relax now; we are safe."

"Words cannot express our gratitude, Lieutenant Kerry," Birdman replied, never taking his eyes off the water. "But I have a job to do, a job that's never done."

Nodding with respect and admiration of the agent's strong

work ethic, Kerry left him to his duties and went to rejoin the others.

Fresh out of cigarettes, Boehner spotted a pack of Kools in one of the scientists' shirt pockets. "You're a true American hero, son," he said with a wink, "but you'd be my own personal hero if you could bum me and the President here a couple of those smokes."

"Speaker Boehner and President Obama," the scientist replied, "to share a smoke with you fellas would be a great honor."

The three men lit up together and engaged in general joviality, looking out upon the water, which was still and almost serene-appearing despite the night's events.

"Mr. President," the Chinese defector said, approaching as he held up his own weather controller. "Now that Jinping's devices are all out of commission, I shall decrease the cloud cover using this."

Obama nodded his approval as the scientist pressed a button. It wasn't moments later before the clouds began to clear and the first rays of sun appeared on the horizon.

"Here, Mr. President," the scientist said, presenting the controller to him. "This now belongs to you."

President Obama took a drag and examined the strange device, mulling over what all he could do with it. "What is your name, sir?" he asked.

"Ping Pong," the scientist replied. "It is my real name, I assure you. Americans give me great tease for it, because same name as table tennis game."

"Well, Dr. Pong," Obama replied, "you're going to be working for me from now on. America is going to be on a new track from here on out, one with a greater focus on funding for science research programs."

Boehner took a deep drag off his Kool. "I gotta agree, Barack," he said. "Though it's known I'm no lover of wasting tax dollars, I can get behind more funding for science if it keeps us competitive with the Chinese, especially after this whole fiasco."

"And we will become more competitive," Obama added. "With the help of people like Dr. Pong here, we can make America a viable nation again in the twenty-first century."

Dr. Pong bowed deeply before the President as Birdman approached from behind, placing a hand on his shoulder. One look at the agent's face told Obama there was trouble.

"What is it, Birdie?" he asked, already suffering the effects of PTSD. "Did I... miss something about this man? Is he dangerous? Damn them, these relentless Chinese!"

"No!" Birdman hissed, glancing nervously about. "No, sir, it's not that. I just, I don't know how else to say this, but... I'm afraid I must... relieve myself... the vice president way? Number two, sir. I gotta go real bad. Will you be safe up here on your own?"

Obama instantly relaxed. "Sorry to ruin the moment," he said, turning back to Dr. Pong. "It's been a rough night...."

Senator Kerry chuckled. "I think between the drones and a guy who won the Purple Heart, that's me by the way, President Obama will be safe. You go ahead. Al Gore brought along his special toilet paper. It's not the best stuff, but it's eco-friendly at least, and it gets the job done. The toilet is just below deck."

"Thank you, Lieutenant Kerry," said Birdman. Obama gave him a nod as he rushed off to do his business.

The two rivals, Obama and Boehner, stood together on deck, surveying the carnage all around them. Both of them took long, satisfying drags off their Kools, leaning on their elbows against the port side railing.

"We're going to do what's right for America," Speaker Boehner offered. "We may have lost a lot of good people tonight, but the thing we should remember is that while they were alive, they really kept us from getting much of anything done around here."

"I completely agree, John. I can say that not only are we going to be good to America, but good to each other from here on out as well." President Obama extended his hand. "Friends, Vice President Boehner?"

"I'd be incredibly honored, sir," Boehner said, taking Obama's hand. "Friends, my dear President."

The two leaders of the Free World shook hands and smiled at each other as water splashed over their faces, extinguishing the cigarettes dangling from their respective lips. Before they could even look up, a forty-five-foot great white descended from its epic leap and bit their enclosed hands off in mid shake.

Everyone onboard was staggered by the attack, the giant shark hitting the side of the boat hard as it splashed back into the water.

Staring at the bloody stumps where their hands used to be, Obama and Boehner exchanged a horrified look before they began to scream. The scientists scrambled for their remotes, sending their drones against this new threat, but there was definitely something different about this shark, almost... uncanny. Not only was this great white somehow capable of dodging their missiles, but it made the previous ones look like runts in comparison.

Looking out across the water, the crew members caught a fleeting glimpse of the gargantuan great white as it passed through their drones' crisscrossing spotlights. An exquisite Chinese flag adorned its dorsal fin, trailing red menace through the water behind it.

This was certainly no ordinary shark. This was a Communist-designed super shark that had swum all the way from Shanghai to Washington in less than an hour.

"No!" cried President Obama, his mouth agape in horror. Through his searing pain, it finally dawned on him what Jinping had meant by the word 'super'.

Wheeling back around for another charge, the man-made Megalodon rammed the Flipper-Flopper at top speed, smashing its hull and spilling almost everyone on deck into the water. Senator Kerry and the entire team of scientists were gobbled up in a matter of seconds, their pilotless drones dropping slowly from the sky.

With President Obama and Vice President Boehner locked firmly in its sights, the super shark swiftly closed in on its prey.

"Please, God!" Obama screamed, doing his best to keep the unconscious Boehner float. "Send this nation a leader who will save us from the shaaaarrr—"

Epilogue

Meanwhile, at the Clinton's Chappaqua estate, the peaceful snoring of three slumbering souls was interrupted by the ringing of Hillary's unlisted cellphone. *Sexy and I know It*, by LMFAO, was her ringtone. She pushed Bill aside and he rolled over, grunting in his sleep, onto a curvy young brunette with a cigar stuck to her thigh.

The well-liked former President spooned the young woman from behind, groping her C-cup breasts while Hilary fumbled for her phone on the nightstand.

"It's late..." she croaked, rubbing her eyes. "This had better be important."

"Secretary Clinton, thank God! Please, listen, I don't have much ti—"

"Hey, do you have any idea what *time it is?*" she snapped, annoyed. "You're interrupting my goddamned beauty sleep!"

Bill took his hand off the young girl's breasts and pulled a pillow over his head. "Who is it..." he mumbled sleepily. "Unless it's those Asian hookers who were supposed to deliver my vegan pad Thai...."

"Ma'am, this is Agent Cardinal," Birdman said. "We *need* you, Secretary Clinton! We need you and all the forces you can muster to the White House right now!"

Bill rolled over and looked at her groggily. "Actually, hun, can you have the hookers bring one of them special vegan pizzas, too?" he asked. "I do so love those. They taste so *real*...."

Hillary placed her hand over the phone. "We'll get some on the way," she said. "We gotta get down to D.C.!"

Bill suddenly sat up. "Is Carlos Danger swinging?! I thought he was supposed to be in New York...."

Hillary shushed him.

"Agent Cardinal," she said, "what has happened to the President?"

"*You're* the president now!" Birdman cried as the Chinese Communist Megalodon closed in on him. "They're all dead!"

"Dead?!" she gasped in response.

"Godspeed, President Clinton, and *save us from this shark!* Oh my god...."

"What's *happening*, Agent Cardinal?!"

"It's having... babies...."

To be continued in Great White House 2: Billary Bites Back

About the Authors

Arthur Graham is a professional editor, writer, and book critic currently residing in Salt Lake City, Utah. He is an accomplished noveler, storyist, and publishite by all accounts. His work has been unfairly compared to that of Charles Bukowski, William S. Burroughs, Hunter S. Thompson, and Kurt Vonnegut, Jr. Once a promising purveyor of fine literary fiction, he has since been reduced to writing about sharks instead. For more of his books and reviews, find him online at Goodreads.com.

Christoph Paul is a musician, podcaster, and YA & Bizarro Fiction author of *The Passion of the Christoph* and *Slasher Camp for Nerd Dorks*, published by Eraserhead Press. He is the co-publisher and editor of New English Press. He plays in rock band Moses Moses & was guitar player/singer of The Only Prescription, but still wishes he was a gangsta rapper. He has even told people he is Drake's full-Jewish brother Rake.

For fun he likes to read YA and Bizarro, get angry in a bar while watching the Miami Dolphins lose, live Tweeting The Bachelor while watching it with his girlfriend, and gardening with his cats. For fun and money he writes Bizarro Erotica under the pen name Mandy De Sandra, who was covered in VICE, Huffington Post, Jezebel, and AV Club.

Sometimes, he dresses up like a famous serial killer and interviews literary types on YouTube.

He is repped by Veronica Park at the Corvisiero Literary Agency.

WALK HAND IN HAND INTO EXTINCTION
Edied by Christoph Paul and Leza Cantoral

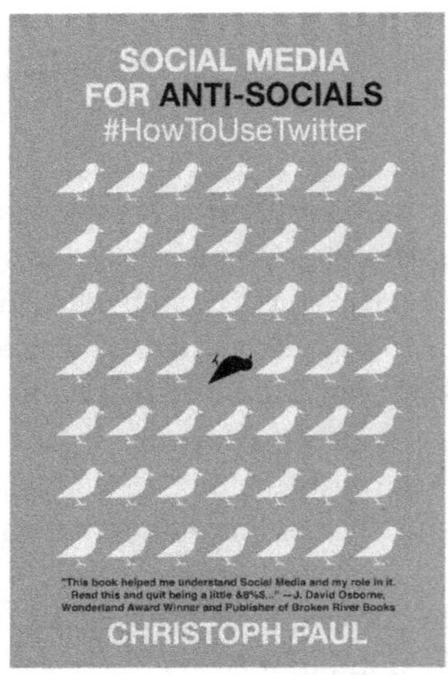

SOCIAL MEDIA FOR ANTI-SOCIALS
by Christoph Paul

SLASHER CAMP FOR NERD DORKS
by Christoph Paul

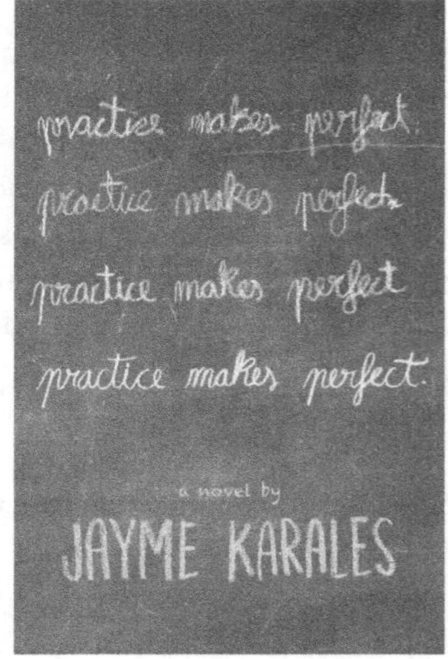

PRACTICE MAKES PERFECT
by Jayme Karales

www.ingramcontent.com/pod-product-compliance
Lightning Source LLC
Chambersburg PA
CBHW060747210726
48292CB00015B/2837